# Springtime on Mars

# Springtime on Mars

Stories

# Susan Woodring

Press 53
Winston-Salem, North Carolina

Press 53
PO Box 30314
Winston-Salem, NC 27130

First Edition

This book is a complete work of fiction. All names, characters, places and incidents are products of the author's imagination. Any resemblances to actual events, places or persons, living or dead, are coincidental.

Copyright © 2008 by Susan Woodring

All rights reserved, including the right of reproduction in whole or in part in any form. For permission, contact author at editor@press53.com, or at the address above.

Cover design by Mendy Mitrani
Cover Photo, "Arlene Janssen, 1959," by George Janssen

"Inertia" previously appeared in *Isotope: a Journal of Literary Nature and Science Writing*, Fall/Winter 2006, and won *Isotope's* 2006 Editor's Prize for Short Fiction

"Radio Vision" previously appeared in *turnrow*, Winter 2007, and won the 2006 Elizabeth Simpson Smith Short Fiction Award

"Springtime on Mars" previously appeared in *Passages North*, Winter/Spring 2007

"The Billy Story" previously appeared in *Yemassee*, Spring 2006

"Love Falling" previously appeared in *Ballyhoo Stories*, Spring 2007

"The Neighbors" previously appeared in *The William and Mary Review*, 2007

"Zenith, 1954" placed 2nd in the 2007 Astrobiology and the Sacred Fiction Competition

Printed on acid-free paper

ISBN 978-0-9816280-0-4

*For my parents*

# Contents

| | |
|---|---|
| Inertia | 11 |
| Morning Again | 25 |
| Beautiful | 45 |
| The Core of Planet Earth | 55 |
| Love Falling | 65 |
| Birds of Illinois | 79 |
| Springtime on Mars | 99 |
| The Billy Story | 117 |
| Radio Vision | 129 |
| Zenith, 1954 | 141 |
| The Neighbors | 157 |

# Acknowledgments

I would first like to thank the good people at Press 53 for their work in putting this book into print. Thank you, Sheryl Monks and Kevin Watson, for your extraordinary care, creativity, and enthusiasm in publishing this collection; you guys are truly a writer's dream.

Thank you to William Donnelly for reading and giving feedback on many of these stories at their beginnings. Ann Hood read and gave invaluable advice on the title story. I am indebted to my writers' group: Priscilla Cutler, Sheryl Monks, Karen McBryde, and Gwynyth Mislin. These dear friends and superb writers read these stories at various stages and gave thoughtful, wise, and encouraging responses. Thank you, Jane McBryde, for allowing us to use your wonderful beach house for our annual retreat— your generous spirit and warmth further endear our meeting place.

No one sacrifices more for my writing than my family. Thank you, Rita and Jerry Sutherland for the cherished gifts of childcare when I most need it, for encouraging me, and for sharing your memories of past events. Thank you to my parents, Bruce and Arlene Yergler, for offering much of the same in terms of caring for my children while I attend book events and for your remembrances of times past. I am grateful to my mother for allowing us to use her photograph in the cover art. And, as always, my husband Danny never tires of bolstering me and keeping my art a priority in terms of time, space, and energy. Thank you so much.

# Inertia

Duncan Jones had thick black lashes and clear blue eyes. His cheeks were fresh pink. He slipped past me at the door and announced he was looking for the lady of the house.

"Is your mother home?" he asked.

I mumbled that she was out back with the bees, and he continued into the house. As he moved across the living room, he paused to touch the papery lampshade on the side table. He fingered the teardrop prism that hung from a string by the window, then glanced at his own reflection in the heavy oak-framed mirror set in the east wall. Duncan was a beautiful boy. He was in the eighth grade, two years older than me, and I was unsure of myself around him. He picked up other things, the ashtray on the coffee table, my grandmother's Hummel figurines on the mantel. Frowning to himself, he held each item in his hand for a moment, as if to ascertain its weight, before returning each to its spot. I stood watching him, slipping my pop-it bracelet off my wrist, working the pops, slipping it back on again. He cocked his head my way for half a second before he returned to the prism and tried to catch a rainbow, but the sunlight was dulled by thick summer clouds and, after holding it this way and that, Duncan released it, freeing the prism to swing wildly for a few seconds before its arc began to slow and narrow.

"Inertia," he said. "It's my favorite force of nature."

I popped-popped-popped my beads and blew a bubble that stretched thin, broke, and stuck to my hair.

"Mine's gravity," I said and collapsed onto the floor. Duncan looked down at me and then away as I lay there, scraping gum off my cheeks. "I love gravity," I told him, giggling to myself, but he wasn't listening to me; he examined a framed photograph of Chestnut Mountain my mother had taken years before. My grandmother had just started living with us when the picture was taken. She and my mother took turns with the camera, taking shots of the mountains, the river, the doe that stepped out of the woods to drink from the stream, then disappeared back into the woods. Duncan looked deep into the picture and squinted at the far-off tree-covered peaks.

A moment later, the back door opened and my mother appeared, her face and arms lightly sunburned, her skirt wrinkled and smudged with dirt. Her hair was frizzy from the humidity and her forehead and chin were shiny with sweat. She said hello to Duncan and invited him to have a seat on the sofa. "We'll all be melting away in this heat," she said, wiping her face with a handkerchief. She patted down her chest and temples and then, looking down to blot the back of her neck, she frowned at my lying on the floor.

"Lizzie-girl, what's this?"

I said nothing, only crawled to the chair opposite the sofa and worked my way up, first gripping the legs of the chair, the seat, finally propping my entire self into the chair while my mother sat composed, her back straight and her ankles crossed, ladylike despite her disheveled appearance. Duncan stood digging something out of his pocket.

"Look," he said, pulling his hand out, fingers closed. He lowered himself onto the couch, next to my mother, turned to face her. "I found it out back behind the railroad tracks." My mother put on an expression of polite interest while Duncan opened his hand before her, his fingers slowly uncurling to reveal a small black stone.

"Where do you think it came from?" he asked.

My mother put out a finger to touch the rock. She had been a science teacher at the high school before I was born and was still widely known throughout town for her fascination with rocks and other specimens from nature. She would lecture anyone who showed even the smallest interest as to the life cycles of moths and honeybees, the formation of rocks and caves. Duncan had brought her a speck of quartz he'd found last summer on a camping trip with his brothers, and before that, dozens of pressed flowers, a few arrowheads, and articles about newly discovered rain forest insects he found in science magazines.

My mother traced the stone's outer edges, an oblong elliptical shape. Her finger grazed Duncan's palm. The stone was thin, a largish button without holes. She asked if she could hold it and Duncan nodded, tipping his hand so that it fell into my mother's palm. She turned it over in her hand and Duncan remained close, their heads bent over his discovery.

"Do you think it's from Earth?" Duncan finally asked.

The air in the room was yellow and thick, too cottony to breathe comfortably. I knew what Duncan was hoping. There had been a UFO sighting recently in New Mexico, and then one just the week before in Montana. Though most people in our town scoffed at these reports, there were some who set out lawn chairs in the evenings and scanned our own skies for the beam of extraterrestrial aircraft. Once, I had a sleepover with a friend whose parents were believers. We were allowed to go out with them. They looked into the vast blankness of space, the stars winking down at them, murmuring to each other about what might descend upon us.

Duncan had brought my mother clippings of both sightings, and watched her scan the articles in much the same way he now watched her assess the stone, turning it over and over again in her hand, studying it. She held it between her thumb and index finger, scrutinizing it by the light from the window. She blew gently across the top of the tiny rock and rubbed it between her fingers.

"Is it from the moon?" Duncan asked.

"It *might* have fallen from the moom," she said after a moment's pause. She smiled at him. "Or it could possibly be a chink from a far-off planet, sent here by a cosmic storm, a gigantic blast across the galaxy." She reached for Duncan's hand, held it palm up, and gently pressed the stone inside.

After Duncan left, she said, "We'll make dinner."

She went to the ice box for pork chops, then turned and looked at me as she sometimes did, like my very existence startled her. "Go after a jar of preserves, Lizzie. And some beans." She brushed a piece of hair from her eyes and turned to set the pork chops on the frying pan; then, noticing me standing still, not moving towards the stairs, she put one hand on my shoulder. "What is it, Lizzie? What's the matter?" She peered down at me, the skin around her eyes pink and creased in white lines. I kept still. "Are you afraid?" She sighed. I smelled the smoke from her beekeeping rising off her hands. I wondered if Duncan Jones had noticed it. Did it intoxicate him as it did the bees? "Are you still afraid of the basement?" she asked.

I didn't answer, wiggling away, her fingers falling off my shoulder as I turned. I stomped down the steps as loudly as I could, but the basement remained nearly soundless, all my thumps echoing hollowly in the solitary room. The shelves on the far wall held my grandmother's canning efforts: tomatoes, okra, peppers; and preserves: strawberry, pear, and rhubarb-strawberry. There were empty spaces now, as there always were this late in the summer, but since my grandmother had passed away last winter, the holes were unsettling. My mother had promised to keep the garden up, but she'd tended only to her bees, poking around in their hives, adjusting the supers and planning out the queen's spots, where each brood would hatch. The hives swarmed twice in the spring. Each time, my mother had planned carefully for the expansion, adding new trays, gently moving the new queen into her own box. I'd asked my mother if she

## Springtime on Mars

wanted some help planting the cucumbers and she stared blankly at me, as if she had forgotten the word's meaning.

She acted as though the basement was a never-ending store of rhubarb preserves, and I wondered if we'd have to replenish it with store-bought tins. My father balked at the idea, saying we would do no such thing. He wanted my mother to face certain realities and called my mother's sudden regular church attendance a phase she would soon abandon, a manner of grieving. The bees were connected to this as well, though he wasn't sure what to make of the long hours she spent in the hives, coaxing the honeycomb out, lifting a gloved hand, covered in bees. He assured me my mother's need to tend to them would pass, the same as people's need to watch the skies for news from other worlds. He taught math at the junior college and this seemed to give him an insight into why people believed what they believed. It's all, he said, an irrational desire to control the uncontrollable. I wanted him to think I had a scientific mind like his, so I nodded and told him I understood, though I didn't.

That night at supper, my father remarked on another UFO sighting, one that had just come out in the evening paper. This time the aliens landed in Germany.

"A man and his little girl saw an enormous frying pan land in a field," he told us partway into our meal. "The spaceship opened and two men in silver suits came out to collect soil samples. The man said he would have thought the whole thing was a dream, but when the flying saucer left, he noted indentions in the ground in the exact position of the base." My father shrugged, taking another helping of green beans. I looked at my mother to see if she might offer information about Duncan's space rock, but she remained quiet, blinking at my father and waiting for him to continue. "It's the Russians, testing aircraft. Some new spying devise, I'd wager. That's what I told Hank." He shook his head, plunging his fork into his green beans. "Hank thinks differently. Says there's something evil afoot."

"The Russians?" my mother asked. She had eaten little and was now fingering the rim of her after-dinner cup of coffee. "What are the Russians doing?"

"Testing aircraft. Covert operations and such. Spy-ware." He spread a generous dollop of rhubarb-strawberry preserves on a slice of bread and nodded at my mother to get him a cup of coffee, but she stared back at him, clearly upset at this new evidence of Soviet mechanical pioneering. "It's not such a surprise, Louise. Our government's up to the same sort of thing. Think of the sightings in New Mexico. What do you think all that is, little green Martians?"

"It could be," I said, speaking for the first time since my mother sent me to the basement. I had eaten little more than she had and was now busy poking holes through a piece of bread. "It's a big universe," I reminded him. "We're hardly the only galaxy around."

My father grinned, winking at my mother who didn't smile back. She hadn't moved to get his coffee, and he pretended not to notice. "Yes, I know it, Lizzie; it is a rather big place, eh? The scope of dimensions known and, what's more, dimensions unknown, is staggering. I'm not ruling anything out." My father was a thin, sandy-colored man who talked with quick, energetic hand gestures. He pointed at me with his butter knife. "To claim that *our* planet holds a monopoly on life would be to grossly underestimate the universe. I like your thinking, Lizzie," he said, and I felt the warmth of his approval spread up the back of my neck.

"Aren't the Russians evil enough?" my mother asked. "Hank said it was something evil. Something more evil than the Russians?"

"There's nothing more evil than the Russians," my father said, smirking.

"You're making fun."

"No, Louise." He paused. "I'm sorry." He reached for his bread, soggy with the preserves from the basement—our quickly dwindling supply—and looked my way. "Lizzie, some coffee please?" I rose to get it for him and he tapped his spoon on the table as he waited. No one spoke as I set the cup before him. Accepting the coffee I brought him, he poured milk into his mug, then stirred slowly. He put the cup to his lips, blew across the top, and set it down again. "You have to admit," he said, "the Communists make a few good points. I'm not saying that I'm communist, just that it's not such a horrible idea. The thought that every person's contribution to society could be equally valued."

"Equally valued?" my mother asked, repeating him, and my father nodded impatiently. She lifted her eyebrows, considering. "My beekeeping is as important as your teaching?"

He flinched. "Your beekeeping is far more important than my teaching."

"You're making fun again," she said, not looking back at him.

"I'm just saying," he turned to me, "that if I were from a galaxy light years away, why would I bother visiting earth? Do you realize what sort of expense that would entail? The years of planning? Of travel?"

"They would do it. If they ran out of sulfur dioxide to breathe." I'd read this in the June issue of *Journey to Worlds Unknown*. Captain Exander had rescued an alien from a dying planet, given the alien pure earth air in his breathing chamber. None of the other planets had the correct, however miniscule, proportions of hydrogen, nitrogen, and sulfur dioxide mingled into everyday breathing air. "People will do anything to sustain their way of life," I said. I'd heard my father make the same comment about the farmers who went for loans at the bank.

He laughed a big and hollow laugh, turning his mug around in his hands. "We're talking about aliens here, not people. Never get the two confused," he answered, smiling into his coffee.

Now he was laughing at me and I couldn't stand it. I glanced quickly at my mother before I blurted out, "They've come. Mom knows it." She looked up, surprised. "Duncan Jones showed us a rock today and Mom said it was from outer space. She said it was a rock from a dying planet, that there are aliens coming. That they are already on their way."

She stared at me as my father shifted in his chair, drinking his coffee. He glanced worriedly at my mother. She had made some effort to tame her frizzy hair with a comb before dinner, but there wasn't much she could do about the sunburn on her cheeks, her nose, the tops of her arms. Since my grandmother died, she had lost weight and there were new hollows at her cheekbones, at her temples. A few red-puckered bee stings were scattered across her arms. Shrinking away from us, she dropped her eyes to the table and wrapped her arms tightly around her chest.

"What's evil?" she asked after a long moment's silence. "What was Hank talking about?"

My father hesitated, looking up at the ceiling and holding onto the table at arm's length, as if for support. He frowned, glancing in my direction, but my mother lifted her eyes, searching for my father's.

"What is it?" she asked.

"He thinks it's the second coming of Christ," he finally answered. "Or rather, he thinks the spacecraft is transporting the anti-Christ. He's calling it the beginning of the thousand-year-reign, or some such nonsense." My father exhaled slowly, then leaned back in his chair to study my mother at a distance. "Really, Louise. What have you been telling these children?"

"The anti-Christ?" she asked. "So soon?"

"Armageddon," my father scoffed.

"The end of the world?"

"Yes." He rose from the table to pour himself more coffee. He stood leaning on the counter with his mug lifted. "It's exactly that, the end of the world." The light outside the window had faded to pink, and though it was still warm, the heat had abated somewhat and I could almost imagine a small breeze through the window. My father sipped his coffee, looking across the kitchen, thinking. When he turned back to my mother, he had softened somewhat, his

shoulders dropped, his face open and soft, wondering. His voice was little more than a whisper.
He asked, "The end of the world—is that what you're afraid of?"

As we prepared for bed, I waited for my mother to scold me for my act of treason. We put out a sheet and some pillows on the rug in the living room since it was the coolest room in the house. My father had taken the electric fan with him into my parents' bedroom. I lay on my back and listened to the summer insects outside the windows, hoping my mother would speak, but she turned her back towards me and was quiet. I watched a spot of light on the wall and imagined the buzzing hives out back in the dark. Only the lesser bees sleep, my mother had told me. I stayed awake for a long time, thinking of the bees.

It was just growing light the next morning when we heard knocking on the front door. It was opened before we could answer, and, seeing us lying on the living room floor, Duncan Jones stepped into the house. He whispered, "They've landed in Germany." He pulled a folded-up newspaper clipping from his back pocket and shook it open. My mother pushed up onto her elbows, but I remained curled up on my side, looking through half-closed lids. "Look, here it is." He held the newspaper up so that, if there had been enough light, we would have been able to read the headline. He knelt in front of us. "Do you know what this means?"

"Duncan," my mother said, sitting up and pulling the sheet around her nightgown. He offered his hand to help her but she managed on her own. "We're not open for company," she said, standing to wrap the sheet more tightly around herself. "You'd better go on home."

She slipped away, into the kitchen, and I grabbed Duncan's hand. "You can stay," I told him. My father was already up, had most likely been up for a while, sitting at the kitchen table, reading the paper and drinking a glass of iced tea. My mother began to move around, gathering eggs and bacon from the ice box, getting the coffee started, and as Duncan stood awkwardly in our living room, him not taking his hand away and yet not folding his fingers around mine, we heard the sounds of breakfast cooking. My father mumbled something about having to stop by the cleaner's in the afternoon and my mother answered by saying not to bother with it, she would pick up his suit when she went to town at noon. "Yes, good," my father murmured absently and, through the doorway, I caught sight of my mother stopping to look out the window. The percolator popped and gurgled.

"Come on," I whispered, pulling Duncan towards the stairs. My nightgown billowed around my hips as I moved. He followed along for a few steps, then glanced back at the kitchen. "Come on," I pleaded. "She has her collection down here."

He finally came with me and together we eased our way quietly down the steps. I reached the light near the bottom and the basement sprang into half-light, gray cinderblock and old boxes. My mother stored our Christmas decorations and a few dusty flower vases down here, but that was all. There wasn't another trace of her, just my father's tool bench, scattered with a hammer and a few screwdrivers he seldom used, a few pieces of discarded furniture, and the jars of vegetables and preserves on the wall. The floor was dirty and wet and the place smelled of mildew and dead insects, thickly settled on the window ledges.

Duncan pulled his hand away. "Well?" he asked. "What collection?"

I pointed to shelves of jams and canned tomatoes. "There," I said, nodding. "Her favorites." He gave me a strange look and so I started to explain to him how important it was for her to tend to the garden, how much she enjoyed cranking up the radio, singing along with Beverly Shay as she set the pressure-boiler up in the kitchen. How she didn't mind the heat and discomfort of a long, late summer afternoon of chopping and boiling and stuffing and sealing, she and my grandmother, together. I spoke quickly and without stopping, trying to stifle the hot ball of anxiety rising in my throat.

"She won first place in bread and butter pickles," I told him. "Three years running."

Duncan shrugged, unimpressed, and turned to go back up the stairs. I came up behind him and took another grab at his hand which he tried to shake away, but I managed to hold on, and with some effort and with the benefit of gravity on my side, I pulled him down, his face close to mine. I meant to place my lips squarely on his, but I had to act fast and so I mostly grazed his sweaty upper lip and nearly kissed his nose. He jerked away and sent me tumbling backwards, crashing onto the concrete floor. I was numb for a moment, unable to move. Duncan stood staring down at me, then shook himself awake and leaned over to help me up.

"Lizzie?" He squinted at me. "Are you okay?"

I rose unsteadily to my feet, leaning on Duncan for support. I was dizzy and sore, my elbows already soft with rising bruises, my head thudding with pain. Duncan watched me, expectant, waiting for me to speak. I sat uneasily on one of the lower steps and brought my hands to my face, finally embarrassed. Tears pricked at the backs of my eyes and I tried to hide them, wiping them away, wishing Duncan away. He stood a few feet back, watching me. I sensed he didn't know if he should stay with me or escape quietly, disappearing out the door with his newspaper clipping, his tiny black rock; maybe he wanted to go look again for my mother, maybe he was afraid to. I wanted to tell him that it was okay, he should leave, but I had given up and was crying too hard now, pushing my hot face against my hands, my shoulders shaking.

He began to step around me and move quietly up the stairs. He put one hand briefly on my shoulder and turned to continue up the stairs when a cry sprang out from above us. Duncan stopped moving. I lifted my face from my hands and looked up. He shook his head, telling me not to speak. There was another cry, my mother calling out something I couldn't quite understand, and then my father's voice, "Louise! Louise, come back here!"

I was the first to reach the top of the stairs, Duncan coming up behind me. My father stood in the kitchen, at the back door, looking out and mumbling to himself.

"She's gone," he said without turning from the screen door. "It's the bees. Do you think I should go after her?"

I stood still for half a beat, not sure what to make of my father's asking me what to do. He looked helpless and small standing there in his navy suit, the tie knotted tight at his throat, his face so cleanly shaven he had a just-plucked look about him. He pulled desperately at his collar and glanced back at me.

"How far will she follow them?" he asked. "Lizzie? How far will she go?"

I pushed past him, stepping onto the porch, and then down the steps. I was halfway across the yard when I heard the screen door clatter shut, Duncan stumbling fast behind me. We both paused at the edge of the yard, looking. Duncan spotted her.

"There," he said.

She was coming to the end of the street, hurrying away, her white nightgown floating behind her, bare feet on the sidewalk. Above her, we saw the cloud of bees pushing through the air like a single animal. The buzzing swarm continued across a well-trimmed yard, over a picnic table, past the filling station at the edge of town. We ran, my mother in front, me and Duncan behind. The buzzing filled my ears. We followed the bees past the railroad tracks, the grain elevator, then onto the highway. They flew among the telephone poles into the cornfields, a vibrating mass. The corn was up beyond our heads and I called out to my mother, afraid she would enter, afraid she would be truly lost, but she kept on the highway, a few cars whizzing past, one car following slowly behind us, my father. The sky was brilliant blue, unusual for summer when there's only the heat, rising like a solid wall all around us, but the air had thinned for us, for our pursuit of the bees. We finally came to a farmhouse, but the bees moved on, and, then, after a plot of soybeans, we came to a small white church, and the bees hovered above, finally alighting on a small red maple at the edge of the lawn. My mother stopped running, and Duncan and I stood a-ways apart from her. My father parked the car. We kept back as the bees covered a tree limb, making it alive, abuzz.

After a moment, the bees began shifting into their upside-down pyramid structure, like something dripping, and my father went to my mother, then reached to touch her shoulder. I couldn't see her face, but I could tell by the way my father moved his hand up and down her back that she was crying. Duncan and I stood back, watching.

# Morning Again

"Harold," I say. "You'd better take me to a rocket launch. I'm sixty-eight years old."

We are sitting down to breakfast in the tiny stucco house I have acquired from my youngest and least grateful child. Dennis is a loan officer at a bank and is privy to reneged mortgages going to auction; he paid for this house in cash and though Harold makes payments for it, Dennis says he wishes he wouldn't. "Let me buy my mother a house," he says. He himself lives in a condo downtown. My other two live in different states but remember to call once a week and don't bother me with crumbling old houses. I am feeling hopeful, though, looking at my plate of fried eggs with the yolks still intact, a cooking grace I seldom manage. I'm clumsy in the kitchen. Two years ago, the president claimed it was morning again in America, and it seems, with that promise still looming over us, that I deserve this; new marriage, new love. Seeing a space rocket tear through the sky then disappear into the blue ought to be my next good fortune.

"Please," I say, sprinkling pepper on my eggs.

"All right, Hon," he says. "We'll do it."

Harold folds up his newspaper and tosses it to a pile on the floor. He is the kind of man who needs that, to fold something up and lay it down, finished, when settling something. We were married three months ago in a small church service and when the pastor proclaimed us husband and wife, Harold's first move was to take my hand and wrap both of his hands around it. It was a sweet gesture, and my children were touched by it, though Harold's children, who are younger than mine, do not seem to take any of Harold's and my attempts at forging a union to heart. They sat there, a son and a daughter with their own children, little ones, gathered to them on those hard pews and gave us small, vague smiles.

His daughter Liza has her problems. She's scary-skinny, wears dark eye make-up, and she always looks confused, as if the normal events and occasions of life are continuously abrupt and foreign to her. She has two children who look simultaneously forlorn and cunning, like they've lost their mother at the supermarket but plan to rob the place in her absence. There's no husband. We had our after-wedding feast, just family, at a country restaurant that serves breakfast all day. Liza stared and stared at her menu. It was mostly pictures, and she seemed intent on studying each one. She was too engrossed to immediately notice her youngest, a boy, rising to stand on his chair and spit milk down at his sister, who was in turn jabbing him in the stomach with her fork. Liza turned her eyes slowly to the boy, finally reaching out a hand to stop him, telling him, weakly, "Sit." Harold won't say it, but I can tell there's something bad wrong with her. She was sixteen years old when her mother died.

The other one, Harold's son, is normal-like. He has a wife and a daughter and a job with Caterpillar, which moved him to Peoria, Illinois several years ago. He kissed my cheek the day I married his father, but it was stiff, and he seemed, throughout the celebration, to be in a grand hurry to get back on an airplane, to shepherd his children away from the South where he himself had once been a child.

I believe: love deep, give marshmallows and other treats to

children, and sleep as long and often as you can, but wake early, eat breakfast. I'm sixty-eight years old; I'm not going backward.

Me and Harold happened quick. I was out bowling with some girlfriends, them laughing because I kept dropping the ball into the gutter. I'm clumsy everywhere. Harold came over to correct my stance, to silhouette my arm to his, to draw my arm back, aim center, let go. I smelled the after-shave on him and I wasn't thinking of his being anyone's father, or having been anyone's husband. We went to Denny's for a late dinner and then out dancing, senior night at a local hotel, and the next day, Sunday, we ate our brunch right here in this tottering old house. We should have known, though, that our past lives would figure into all of this. When you get to be a certain age, you are no longer you but rather a conglomeration of people and dates and events. You are a country, complete with history and song.

"When will you take me?" I ask, still admiring my sparsely peppered eggs, twin suns. I could take a picture, they're so lovely. "There will be one in January," I tell him.

Harold picks up his coffee cup and looks at his empty plate. I can tell he misses the paper he's just discarded, and I reach down for it, set it back in front of him. He gazes out the window behind me, saying nothing about my not yet eating my eggs, which is the opposite of what my ex-husband would do. It annoyed him for me to enjoy a simple thing, a thing apart from him, and it frightened him, too, how little I needed.

"It's the one with the teacher," I say.

"A teacher in space," he says. He finishes his coffee and sets the cup down for me to take to the sink and rinse. "A teacher gone astronaut," he says. He has told me of the summer he and his first wife, Marjorie, took their children to see Apollo lift off in one of its later moon missions. *It shot off clear to the moon,* he told me, and I pictured him standing in a patch of sandy grass in Florida, his kids jumping and pointing, Marjorie at his side. Harold kept sight of the shuttle as it burst upwards, soared across, traveling that great distance in one terrific zip. "We might be next," he jokes, tapping his fingers to the table. "Maybe they need some old people. For our experience. You and me, Hon, to the moon."

It's October now; the launch will be in three months. I consider that—we're three months into marriage, and in another three, we'll drive down to Cocoa Beach in Florida and that will be our first half-year.

"We'll go there together," I say.

"Right-o," Harold says, rising and stretching, glancing at the oven clock. He is retired from a career of selling bath fixtures in a department store, but he is working again now, part-time at a house wares retailer. There, he moves merchandise around on a forklift. Though my children are older, it's because I got started earlier; Harold is seventy-four. "We'll make a plan."

Halloween comes, me handing out fistfuls of candy to the neighborhood children, and then Thanksgiving supper which my middle child drives down to cook. At Christmas, Harold's daughter Liza does not visit but Harold goes and gets her kids and we plan to have them stay with us a few days. My oldest daughter comes, and Harold's son sends us fruit.

For New Year's, we have Liza's kids again. The girl, Shannon, is twelve and she sits on the couch, enduring the endless Rose Bowl parade on the television, perking up a little when I bring out popcorn. She paints her fingernails in the bathroom and is messy with the polish on the counter. Then, once her nails are dry, she sets about scraping the polish off with her teeth. Specks of gnawed pink litter the carpet. The boy Trent, seven years old, plays with his cars and watches football with Harold. Sometimes, he puts the cars in the toilet and me or Harold have to go and fish them out. It angers Harold, but I keep him from yelling—what good would it do? I stop myself from pointing out that the child has not been taught better.

When it's almost time to take them back, we receive a phone

call from a nurse in the town they live in, and she tells us to keep them a bit longer. Their mother is in the hospital, recuperating from a car accident. Liza hit the side of a bridge; the car was smashed up bad, but mercifully, she came away with only a few scrapes and a broken arm.

I tell Harold the next morning, "I love these children."

"I know," he says. He was up late, talking to his son on the telephone, and his face is gray, his eyes weak-looking. We are eating dinner rolls with jelly and speaking soft, so the children, asleep down the hall, won't hear. The house feels more run-down now with Harold's grandchildren here, their things lying about. Teen heart-throb magazines and playing cards and the boy's discarded underwear. Little Trent strips down to nothing, then watches television, plays with his cars. We have our days and nights: days, the children are awake, the girl traipsing through, the loose hem on her nightgown skimming the carpet, her blinking quickly, as if she is always trying to come to, to arouse her thoughts, the boy dribbling chocolate milk and shooting at things with an invisible gun; nights and early mornings, the children are asleep and there is some peace, though the frayed nightgown, the invisible guns are pending—there is energy and disruption awaiting us.

"We'll see her, when we bring the kids back. We'll see if we can't help," I say.

Harold nods. He's told me that he endured long years, hoping his children would grow up. He confessed: after his wife died, he marched them through school, through summers and sports and part-time jobs, always waiting, longing, for the moment he would be free. I love Harold for saying it—it's not many of us who will tell such a hard truth—and I pity him. I would relive every minute of my own children's growing up if I could.

"We will help her," I promise.

The latter part of January comes, and Liza is yet not ready to have the children returned. I worry over the children's schooling, but Harold won't hear me. He says they'll be back home soon enough and if they have to repeat the grade, it'll likely do them good anyway. I ask Shannon if she misses her mother, and she only shrugs. Trent pulls back the elastic band of the underwear he's just taken off and shoots it across the room. I tell my daughter on the telephone, "This is a sad case."

I make preparations for our trip—the children will come with us. Taking Trent aside, I explain to him that if he brings a toy car into a service station and drops it in one of those hell-hole commodes, neither his grandfather nor I will get it out for him. "So, don't try it," I say. His sister, who is not supposed to hear but does, snickers and I warn her with this: "You will say please and thank you and you will every once in a while smile in your grandfather's presence or else I'll cook you a meatloaf the second we return home. I'll cook it and I'll cook it badly, and it will be raw or burnt or both and you will have to eat it anyway." Her lips form the word *gross,* but she says nothing and her eyes go, for a moment, as vacant as her mother's.

To ready the children for the trip and because they're missing school, I educate them on space travel. While Harold is at work, I sit them at the kitchen table and give Trent a sheet of typing paper and a new package of crayons and Shannon a spiral-bound notebook and a green ink pen. I tell the boy to draw a space rocket and spell the word *Sputnik* for him, explaining that it's Russian for rocket. I instruct Shannon, "Take notes." She pauses chewing on her fingernails to stare at me, as if I'm speaking some language she's never heard of, and I tell her again, "You'll need to write this down. First, 1957. We heard about Sputnik on the news and we went outside to watch it shoot through the sky, launched all the way from Russia. *Russia.* We didn't know a thing about Russia then. We still don't. I was already a married woman in middle life and I tried to imagine how nation-proud the average Russian woman was, but I could not—I knew nothing about Russia except it is cold there, the men drink vast amounts of vodka, and everyone eats black bread and cabbage soup. My middle child, my youngest girl, was eleven. And Dennis, my baby, was nine. I bought him a toy space rocket and he launched it in the back yard. It was a cold fall; we had early snow.

"This was the beginning of the space race. The Russians launched Sputnik; that was 1957. In 1969, we put a man on the moon and won the race. By then, Dennis was twenty-one, finishing up college, and my older two were already married. Becky, my oldest, had a baby. The baby was just walking then. Her father, who is rude, made a joke of the baby walking better than those fruity astronauts. Off wasting our money, he said. Most people were amazed at the moon-landing, but there were nay-sayers. You will always have people such as these, the people who don't believe in *anything*."

I look at the children. Trent has drawn a race car, named Sputnik, and Shannon is playing, trying to recap her pen without actually touching the cap, instead nosing the tip of the pen inside it, pushing it against the table. She has not written a word.

"In Vietnam," she says, "they eat monkey brains."

Later, we go looking through Harold's boxes because I want to show the children pictures of their mother from when she was young. It is a brittle winter day and the house is too quiet; I fear Harold's too-early return. He has all of his clothes, mostly button-downs made of thin material and stiff blue jeans, hanging in the closet in our bedroom, his t-shirts, socks, and underwear and neatly folded and placed, by me, in two dresser drawers. When he moved in all the way, giving up his old place, he took a few unmarked cardboard boxes and put them up in a separate closet, the one in the house's second bedroom, where the children are staying now. I haven't before looked inside these boxes and Harold has never volunteered to tell me about them. The children are at my elbows as I open the closet door. There are just three, in a row at the bottom. The closet is otherwise empty, save a few empty hangers and a rain jacket hanging on a hook on the door. Without a word, I settle on the floor and open the first one.

I've told Harold everything there is to know about my life. During our early bowling days, we stayed up late in my kitchen, talking, me telling him about my girlhood years in Benton where my daddy was a machinist at the furniture plant and my mother stayed home and tended babies. I married my first husband Robert when he was in school to become a teacher; he dropped out his second year to take a job with a bank. He turned money-crazy, even though we didn't have any. *Especially* because we didn't have any. Here, Harold set his glass of iced tea and whiskey down and crossed his arms. I told him: I made up my own world, just me and my babies. I never ventured out of that world, never thought I'd have a need to. The children were already grown when Robert's girlfriend called me to tell me of her existence. I packed my clothes, took five hundred dollars from our savings account, and Dennis bought me this house. "The rest," I told Harold, "I did on my own."

Harold responded with trifles. He told me of summer vacations, counting them off on his palm and squinting to remember. In 1960, they went to Myrtle Beach. Liza was six already then; the baby, Harold's uppity son, was a year old. Nineteen sixty-one, the mountains. Nineteen sixty-two, Marjorie's family reunion in Jackson. Nineteen sixty-three, the beach again. Nineteen sixty-four, Philadelphia, so that the children could see the liberty bell. In 1970, they made a cross-country trip to see Yellowstone and the Grand Canyon. Mount Rushmore. "Magnificent," Harold told me. There was nothing of his meeting his wife, and nothing of the time before or after her. Even the vacation recaps were of only the places they'd seen, the accommodations, the restaurants, the camp grounds. I asked him, "What about your wife?" And he said, "Her name was Marjorie." That was all.

The first box is full of papers; there's a pink carbon of a life insurance policy on top. I place it aside, and Shannon picks it up to look at it but doesn't comment. Next, a stack of pay stubs, from the department store Harold used to work at. There are mounds of these, held together with rubberbands. They date back to the early fifties, when Harold first started working there. I show Shannon the amount, a hundred and forty-six dollars. Trent says, "Whoa," and I don't know if it's because he thinks a hundred and forty-six dollars is a lot of money or if he knows how little it is, how little it will buy you. He is only seven, though, and by the time I reach the bank statements at the bottom of the box, he is gone, wiggled under the bed and talking to some imaginary war creature hiding there. Shannon and I are left.

"We'll close this one," I say, and she nods. She has, at least for the moment, arisen from her adolescent stupor, and she gestures to the next box. I open it, and she looks inside, lifts at a photo album which looks a few decades old, but it's stiff to open, and photographs fall out, onto her lap. The pages of the album are clean, unused.

"She never got to it," I say. "She never got them put in the pages."

"Who?" Shannon shakes her bangs from her eyes, looks at me.

I'm about to say Marjorie, but I don't. "Your grandmother," I say, and Shannon shrugs, which I've come to see is something she does when she doesn't want anyone to know she doesn't completely understand, or that she is not sure what is required of her. "Your mama's mama," I say, picking up the photographs.

They're the muted square color pictures of the '60's and '70's, those colormatic years. Badly done, some fuzzy, others overexposed or taken in darkness, the pictures are full of shadows, but I study each one, engrossed. It's like passing into the closed-off spaces of Harold's life story, looking through them, seeing his boy, young and blond with hair that has grown past his collar, walking someplace sunny, grimacing at the camera. There, a girl on the beach, Liza. She is wearing a dark swimsuit and a straw hat, and is giving the camera a pouting, put-off look, her solitude just disrupted. She is young here, maybe just a year or two older than her daughter now, looking on. Shannon stares, wordless, at the photo. I know what she sees, because it's the same thing I'm looking at—here, Liza, though turning away from the camera, has a clear look in her eyes. Her face is open and natural and looking into the world as if she knows what it holds for her, like she is not afraid or confused by it. As if, were she to dive into the greenish-blue ocean behind her, she would emerge strong and material, water glittering gold on her skin. This girl might smile, as free as sunshine.

"I thought *you* were my grandmother," Shannon says.

I don't believe she really thinks this way, but I answer her plainly. "You had a grandmother before me." I uncover another photo, one of Harold with dark, full hair, a grim smile, wearing the sort of vacation-wear—shorts, aqua button-down—I never would've imagined him capable of. Maybe I would have, though, if I'd really thought about it, imagined it—Harold *had* been young; in my hands lie the proof. "Your grandfather." I pass it to her. Then another: a shot of a woman with dark hair blowing into her face, her standing with her arms hugged to her in a windy patch of country, a red-leaved autumn tree behind her.

"Here," I say, pointing. "Here is your grandmother. Her name was Marjorie."

She looks at the photo, studying it with interest. "If she were still alive, you wouldn't be here," she says. "I wouldn't even know you. *None* of us would." She pauses. "If my mother didn't drive like a maniac, me and Trent would be back at home." She fingers the photo. "If she could just keep her car on the road," she says.

I say nothing to this, only pack up the box, slide it back into its place, shut the closet door. When my oldest, Becky, was a teenager, she tried out for cheerleading and lost out. She played the what-if game for days, going through the scenarios: if she'd practiced her round-off a few more times, if Darcy Anson had not taken her spot in line, if her hair was long enough to go into a ponytail. Becky talked it out this way, working it out while I was preparing dinner, stirring spaghetti sauce in one pot, trying to keep the noodles from sticking in another. She never spoke word one of it to her father except to say she guessed they had an IQ requirement, and hers was way too high. Becky laughed, and waited for Robert to laugh with her. She was looking for something else from her father, though, some show of hero, and she didn't get it—he only chuckled, said, that's my girl.

"Once, she knocked down an entire row of mailboxes." Shannon rises, stretching. She sits on her unmade bed, her legs dangling off the end. "It's her eyes. She probably just needs glasses."

"Whatever it is," I tell her, repacking the box, "it's not because of you, not because of your brother. Whatever it is that makes her drive crazy, it's something else, something that has nothing to do with the two of you."

I stand, sit next to her on the bed, and touch her shoulder. She flinches a little but I can tell she's trying not to, that she wants to let me comfort her, and in the same moment, she also wants to flee.

On our way to Florida, I read aloud from the Sunday paper special insert: "Christa McAuliffe was born in Boston, Massachusetts." The whole country is talking about her. "Her husband is a lawyer. She wants to touch the future. Judith Resnik," I say, gleaning information from the article, "is a real astronaut. She got a perfect score on her SATs. Ronald McNair, the black one, will play the saxophone in space." I turn back in my seat to look at Shannon. "Have you taken your SATs yet?"

For a long moment, she says nothing, the four of us bumping along 85 southbound for Cocoa Beach, where we'll park early in the morning, waiting for the launch. We've just entered South Carolina and the weather is gray. I hope the sun will burn through; it's early yet. The boy spent the first hour knocking his race cars against the window, but now he's asleep, his mouth agape, and I catch Shannon tossing bits of cotton candy into the opening, with modest success. "It'll make his drool pink," she says.

I made her stop, and she gives me a look—I don't know how things are between us. Since we opened the boxes and she told me about her mother's clumsy driving habits, she's been at odds compliant and mean, washing dishes with me after dinner, telling me of a television show she loves, one where green slime oozes down from above onto the characters' heads, their shoulders, while other times, she stomps about the house; she smeared peanut butter on the lenses of my reading glasses. Harold wanted to tear her up for that, said it was about time, but I held him back, told Shannon to clean them, we'd be good then. She hasn't told Harold what we found in the boxes, that we went looking, and neither has Trent, though I'm yet afraid I'll get caught. I want to tell Harold the truth, to right things, but I'm afraid of the space it will make between us. He'll be angry, at first, to know I went snooping through his things, that I invited his deviant grandchildren along in my nosiness, but he'll forgive me that. Harold is a forgiver. My true offense: he'll know I know something of Marjorie. I don't know if he can stand it, me knowing just that much, what she looked like.

"I'm twelve," Shannon says, unnecessarily. I wonder if this is prelude to some important declaration, some freedom that ought to be granted her, or just the realization of only that—her age. She yet has her vacant moments, and this might just be her arising, remembering herself.

"Yes," I say. "We know, honey."

"You don't take the SAT until you're sixteen."

Harold says, abruptly, "Why are they going? I mean, what do they plan to do up there?"

I scan the article. "It says here they will deploy a satellite. They always deploy satellites, I guess. And, also, launch a module to observe and collect data on the tail of Halley's Comet. It's an educational experiment, too. Christa McAuliffe will teach from space. Gravity. The density of earthly items in a no-atmosphere state."

"Fun," Harold says, waving his hand. "They are going for *fun.*"

It's mid-Monday morning; the traffic is steady but not heavy and the sky has cleared, the sun showing itself now, rising to just above Harold's chin through his window. We're in Harold's Cadillac, a long white embattled vessel that looks like an historic relic from the outside and smells like cough drops and wet paper towels on the inside. I'm surprised to hear this from Harold and am brought back to my son-in-law who made jokes about man's first walk on the moon. My son-in-law is now an orthodontist, and he makes good money, but he was wrong about disbelieving the moon. Now, here's Harold, speaking in a tone of voice I've only heard him use a handful of times—once about a member of our local school board who wants to remove the word *hatred* from the high school history books.

"Fun and games," he says.

"Why are *we* going?"

This comes from Shannon in the back seat. I turn to glance at her. She has the dull-eyed, slightly greasy look of a person on a long car trip. She looks dispassionately back at me. We have all day to go yet.

Trent wakes, rubbing his nose, and starts to cry. He's wiping the pink goo from his chin. Shannon stares at him as if she doesn't know where he's come from, as if she's never seen him before.

"Ooh," she says. "Yuck."

"For fun," I say, handing him a tissue. I sound too serious, and I try to lighten my tone. "And for educational purposes."

We make it to Georgia. I'm telling stories of when my three were little, the scrapes they got into, and I mean for these to be inspirational anecdotes—how to go on when your best friend drops you cold in the middle of band competition weekend, what to use in the place of glue when you run out the night before your science project is due—but when we pull off the interstate for lunch, Shannon says, "Free at last," rather dramatically, and I see Harold smile.

At the table, Trent immediately dumps the golf tees from the brainteaser the restaurant has provided us, to wile away our time while waiting for our bowls of soup, and Shannon studies the menu. "I hate everything," she says, and I expect Harold to be annoyed with her, but he is yet amused by her free-at-last comment, and he laughs instead.

"Let's just go back home," she says.

"You can do that, young lady," he says. "Good luck thumbing."

Shannon shrugs, then gathers up the tees which Trent has been lining up, balancing them on their heads, across the edge of the table in front of him. He protests, but she ignores him and he comes around the table, settling onto my lap. I smooth his hair.

She puts the tees in their holes. It's a triangular-shaped piece of wood with enough tees for all of the holes but one. The game is to jump the tees across each other and take them out, like checkers, until you're stuck. There's a key to tell you your intelligence—one is genius-level; twenty is moron.

"Come on, Jean," she says. "Try it."

I glance at Harold who isn't even paying attention. He's instead looking out the window, drinking his coffee. So far, that's all we've gotten—coffee. The place is nearly dead—nearly, not all the way, because a Cracker Barrel Restaurant is never *all* the way dead—and our waitress can't seem to find our table, to take our order. Harold sniffs; he's fiddling with his sunglasses. Trent puts his head against my collar-bone.

"You try," I tell her. "Give it a whirl."

She won't, though, and Trent, lifting his head, announces he has to use the bathroom. "I gotta pee," he says, though he's already been; the first thing we did when we entered was march both children to the restrooms. Harold takes him, though. His mood is upbeat now; the traffic has been good.

"Go on," Shannon says, the boys gone, her still urging me to take a turn at the wooden triangle I.Q. test.

"I've raised three children," I tell her.

Shannon is unimpressed. "Try the test," she says, grinning, as if I've already registered moron.

By a miracle, our waitress appears. She's a heavy woman with a plain, unadorned face who regards us cheerfully but efficiently, takes our order, and promises to be back. "Go *on,*" Shannon says, pushing the triangle towards me.

"These puzzles don't show a thing. My Dennis could always do it, and you know how smart he is." I laugh. Shannon's looking at me; of course, she has no idea how smart Dennis is. "Well," I say with a sigh, "actually, he *is* smart. But not that that matters. He can't keep a wife, has no children. His job requires him to judge people by the amount of money they have in their bank accounts. You pass or fail," I say, nodding, "in Dennis's book, by your bottom line. Net worth."

"Try."

I can tell when a person starts to hate someone. Before I even knew about the other woman, one morning I woke up in bed and turned to stare at a familiar sight—the back of Robert's bare shoulders just above the covers, him turned on his side away from me. I'd seen those shoulders a million times, and I'd always before felt an impulse to reach out to touch that bit of pale flesh, sprinkled with tiny moles. I'd wanted to touch those shoulders even though they weren't the shoulders of a Hollywood leading man, even though they weren't particularly strong. I'd wanted to reach out, lay a hand on them or the hollow space in between, the center, every morning in my whole married life, except this one. I lay there a long time, wondering at my sudden hatred. Robert woke up, slipped out of bed and padded across to the bathroom in his underwear, and he didn't notice how I'd changed. In a marriage, you can have one who doesn't love the other, if only for a time. It often is this way: love wanes, it waxes once again. But for both to be done with it at the same time is the real trouble.

Shannon is giving me a half-smile, and I see it clear—she hates me. And, as soon as I see that, I also see a reason for it: it's because I know. I have spoken directly of her mother's trouble and now, this girl, in her twelve years, in her stringy hair and gnarled nail polish, hates me.

"Try it," she says. "Just *try.*"

Harold and Trent are gone for such a long time, I run out of hesitations and choose my first tee. "These games don't mean anything," I say, jumping another tee, removing it from the board. There's a trick to it: start in the middle and go around, spiral out. The waitress returns with our drinks; I explain the boys are not returned yet and she leaves. "There's no way to tell a person's intelligence," I tell Shannon. "Only by their actions. Actions are all that count." I wonder if Harold and Trent have wandered off to the gift shop, or if Trent has removed every article of his clothing, if he's shoved it all down the toilet. I wish they'd return. "A person is as a person does," I say, and make a second, a third move.

"We're not going to the launch," Shannon says. "Watch and see. We won't."

"What do you mean, not go?" I ask. "What are you talking about?"

She shrugs and grins and then nods at Harold, who I can see returning to our table. He's carrying Trent, coming from the bathroom, making his way through the maze of tables and chairs, waitresses and diners. Next, Harold is standing at the table, Trent in his arms looking tiny and white, completely dressed. He's obviously sick, though, his eyes dark. Harold says, "He's feeling puny." I rise to touch his little-boy cheek, and we gather our things, leave a few dollars to pay for the sodas, Shannon skipping out into the parking lot, her hair loose in the chilly air.

Harold may have taken his first wife to see Apollo rocket into outer space, but I'll have to settle for a double-bed room at a motel in East Bridge, Georgia with a puking seven-year-old boy and an adolescent girl who says, happily, "Back on the bus, y'all."

The afternoon is stuffy and too-warm in our orange-toned room, me holding a trashcan for Trent, Shannon flipping the channels. Harold sits on the one chair in the room, looking through a part in the dense curtains through the window. Shannon says she hates everything, again, like she did at the restaurant, until she finds a cartoon. Both children fall asleep after a while, and I wipe Trent's face with a washcloth and tuck Shannon in.

Settling on an edge of bed across from Harold, I tell him, "I looked through your pictures. In the boxes. I saw your wife. I saw a picture of Marjorie, and she's beautiful."

He closes his eyes and says nothing, though I can tell he's heard me. After a time, he says, "Jean. *You* are my wife."

In the night, I don't sleep for rethinking it, for saying it again and again to myself, me even hazarding to whisper it aloud, the words spoken out into the gray motel room, among the sounds of sleeping and the heater clicking on and off, the sound of cars stopping and doors slamming; it is the kind of motel that takes lodgers in at all hours of the night. "Jean," he says, "*you* are my wife."

In the morning, Trent is better, and Shannon has put her vacant look back on, no longer hating or even acknowledging me. We resume our places in the Cadillac. There's not enough time to get to Cocoa Beach in time for the launch, but we drive on, southward, see how close we can get. I try to get Shannon talking about cheerleading, Trent about monster trucks, but they're both worn out by the trip, by Trent's sickness, and they hardly answer me. Harold whistles a little, absently.

We get as far as Port Orange when the radio starts to give the two-minute countdown. The announcer tells of the last checks, the firing spots in place, the weather, cold and clear. We pull over and stand in the weeds at the side of the interstate, Harold pointing the direction out, the piece of sky to watch. The radio is on inside the car, but we can't hear it, so Trent gives us the final countdown, ten, nine, eight, hoping to see the lift-off when he gets there, starting again at ten when it doesn't happen. Finally, "There!" Shannon calls, pointing, and we catch the sight of the shuttle thrust, us witnessing the steady stripe of white lead into the sky. There's the shuttle, and I think: there are *people* inside. The wind is chilly but not unpleasant, and the sun is almost all the way up; it's eleven-thirty in the morning. I keep watching, though I feel the children already shifting, bored that easy; the rocket has launched and they're ready to get back in the car, face the long drive back. I keep my eyes turned upward, though, and I see it happen, see the tiny spot in the sky turn to fire, smoke, *gone,* and Harold's there in a second, his hand on my back. We look hard, until our eyes hurt from the sun, us trying to figure why they have done it, and it's only after several long moments that we begin to say the word *accident,* then, *explosion.*

The next morning, back home, we see the recorded launch on television; the morning shows are replaying it, parsing the disaster, already searching for meaning. Instinct, I guess. The announcers, the NASA officials, and various politicians make nonsense noises about what's happened, because they don't know—the brainteaser, the photo albums, the rocket experts, my perfect sunny yellow eggs, none of it tells anyone a single thing. These things make no real promises, offer no predictable warnings. I grip Harold's hand and watch the shuttle disappear into a y-shaped plume of smoke again and again until my eyes are raw from crying. Trent doesn't pay attention; he's already back to zipping about in the buff, but Shannon sits biting her fingernails on the couch and glances, every few moments, to the telephone on the kitchen wall. I can't say if we're lucky or not, if we missed something we should have seen or if we got off easy, viewing it from afar, removed. After a long time, though, I move to switch off the television, lead Shannon into the bathroom, sprinkle polish remover on a cotton ball.

I take her hand and begin work on her thumb. I tell her, "When I was a girl, there was little talk about space travel. People spoke of going to the moon, to other planets, but they didn't believe it would really happen." I swipe the polish off, turn the cotton ball over to start her index finger. "They never believed any of this could happen."

# Beautiful

Joel lay on the ugly pheasant-patterned spread and thought about the things he wanted to tell Mary. She had promised to bring the girls up next weekend. He watched television with the sound turned off and sipped berry-flavored wine from a disposable cup. The hotel room wall was washed yellow from the light fixture in the bathroom. Above him, on the otherwise whitish ceiling, there was a Kentucky-shaped water stain.

He was growing weary of hotel-life. Early in his stay, he had encountered an older couple from Illinois who was visiting their son in Greensboro. "His wife," the woman told Joel on the elevator, "won't let us stay with them." The man put in, "Our son is a doctor." He had also met a middle-aged biker couple who took bananas and yogurt from the continental breakfast up to their room, and an outdoor lighting salesman from Virginia. One evening, Joel and the salesman drank a couple of beers together by the pool. "I hate these kinds of places," the salesman said. "Too many kids and crackpots." The biker couple sat across the pool from them, peeling oranges and dropping the rinds into a six-pack sized cooler. The woman wore a black bra visible through her white blouse, sleeves rolled up to reveal the loose flesh on her arms. Catching Joel's eye, she smiled at him. The salesman grunted, tipping back his beer.

He was staying there for work, on an eight-week contract as a biomedical technician in the nearby hospital. He spent most of his evenings watching television and thinking about Mary and the girls or else he opened one of the adult magazines he kept in the nightstand, tucked under the greater Greensboro area phone book. The curious thing about this hotel room was that he had not been able to find the Gideon's Bible. He wondered if a previous guest had stolen it. Joel planned to throw the magazines out before Mary came, and then he would not buy any more. Sometimes, the hotel manager, a small dark-skinned man who spoke with a foreign accent Joel couldn't place, gave him a sort of cozy smile when Joel came down in the mornings, and he wondered if the manager looked through his things while he was at work. Maybe he had swiped the Bible himself. When Joel's contract was up, he may have to sign on for another stint. He hoped to return home instead.

He had vague, hopeful thoughts about his life with Mary and the girls. He planned to take them on a trip to Hawaii someday. His credit card had a plan for earning air travel miles and discounts at hotels. He wanted to take his family to a luau, for them to sit around a pig pit watching hula dancers and fire eaters. Such an escape, he imagined, would be good for all of them.

They came on Friday, in time for dinner and he took them to the pizza place across the street. Mary wore a soft blue blouse Joel didn't remember seeing before. The girls were still tan from the summer, their long blonde hair identical in color and length, though the youngest, Jamie, rarely bothered combing hers. Hillary sat next to Joel and stared at the spaces between the booths, as if she were waiting for someone more interesting to join them. Her fingernails were colored purple with a felt-tip marker. Jamie sat across from him, next to her mother.

The waitress brought their sodas, and Joel asked, "So, girls. What's new?" He turned to Hillary. "Hill?"

"Nothing," she answered flatly. "Everything's perfect."

## Springtime on Mars

Jamie tapped a breadstick into the foil ashtray. "I beat up this boy named Derek Matthews at school today." She examined the end of her breadstick, then took a bite. "He had it coming."

"Just perfect," Hillary said.

"I grounded her," Mary put in. She looked at Joel. "The school called and I grounded her. Except for this weekend, except for this." She lifted her hands to indicate the pizza restaurant, the trip to North Carolina. "We can't cancel *this*." Mary paused. "I'm sorry," she said. "Really. This is good." She nodded to herself, and, looking up, to Joel. Jamie laid her palm flat on the table and spread her fingers out, then bopped them one at a time with her other fist. "This weekend is necessary," Mary said, "for all of us." She directed her last words at Hillary who huffed a little, rolling her eyes, and Joel understood there had been some discussion over their coming, that Mary had made her come. Mary rubbed her hands together. She looked embarrassed, like she was unsure of how to be normal with Joel there, and he wanted to keep her from feeling that way.

"Mary," Joel said.

"Stop." She held up her hand. Hillary glanced at her mother, then away. There had been some trouble with her and a high school boy and now she could not look her father in the eye. When she was little, though, she used to cup his face in her hands and draw it very close to her own. *Listen,* she would say. *There's a crisis on planet Gimbel and we have to go there now.* Joel thought of the ugly bedspread, his space away from Mary and the girls. Mary had insisted on their staying in different rooms for this visit, but Joel had hoped she would change her mind. He had thrown the magazines away; the Bible was still missing. He should replace it. He wanted to tell Mary about that, about how he would go out to one of those Christian bookstores. He thought there were a lot of them in the area; he wanted to tell Mary that, too.

"Mary," Joel started again, but she shook her head.

"So happy," Hillary said, and Joel turned to her, where she sat next to him, but her eyes didn't even flicker his way. He touched her leg, just gently, under the table, and she shifted away.

"Now, listen," Joel said, but then floundered, unable to think what else to say.

"A kick to the gut," Jamie said. "I clobbered him."

The restaurant was too warm and full of the hum of conversation, diners laughing and talking over their greasy pizzas. Mary was better at holding people close. She still kept in touch with their neighbors after they moved away, even sent Christmas cards to some of the girls' former teachers. He watched his wife pulling at a loose thread in her sleeve and Hillary peering down at her purple fingernails, no longer interested in interplanetary travel, in holding his face still while she talked to him. *Listen,* Joel remembered.

"What did he do?" he asked suddenly. He was looking at Jamie, but also taking in Hillary's stubborn quiet, Mary's weariness. "You said he had it coming. Well, what did he do?"

Jamie slumped down in the booth next to her mother, and said, "He told a lie about me." Joel kept looking at her, waiting. Mary leaned closer, squinting. Whatever the boy had said, she had not yet told her mother. "It was a thing that wasn't true."

"What was it?" Joel asked. "Tell us, Jamie."

"He said I was ugly," Jamie answered after a pause. Mary touched her arm, glancing at Joel in an involuntary way, a tiny gasp, and she corrected her gaze, settling again on Jamie. "That's not true," Jamie said. Hillary's face softened a little, looking at her sister.

"Of course it isn't," Joel said. He wanted to reach across the table to her, to gather all three of them to him. "You're beautiful girls, both of you." Jamie shook her tangled hair out of her eyes, and Hillary went back to staring ahead, ignoring him. "Just beautiful," he said.

They returned to the hotel where Mary and the girls checked into their room and went up to put their swimsuits on. Joel changed quickly in his own room and took the elevator to the first floor. He chose a lounge chair and sat waiting for his family.

The pool was crowded with teenaged girls—a soccer team from a high school in Alabama, he heard one of the adults yell to another above the din of the girls' screeches bouncing off the fogged windows, the wet tile. The damp air was full of the smell of chlorine and mildew. An attractive woman in ripped jeans and a tank top sat poolside with a beer; next to her was a frumpy-looking woman sipping a diet soda. The ugly one was talking on and on, the pretty one nodding and gazing out at the girls splashing and yelling in the water. A pregnant woman stood in the shallow end amid the screeching soccer players. She beckoned a small girl in a pink bathing suit to jump to her. At the deep end, a young black couple sat on the edge with their feet in the water. The man had a trim mustache and the woman wore a bikini with a tiny silver ring glinting from her belly-button. She pulled her arms over her head to stretch, her smooth brown belly pulled taut. After a moment, the little girl in the pink suit jumped to her mother, and, a few minutes after that, the soccer team was called out by the diet-soda mom.

Mary and the girls appeared then, Mary in a long button-down shirt over her tropical-flower suit, the girls with hotel towels gathered around them. Joel saw Hillary watching the teenagers pulling themselves out of the pool, water dripping from their bony frames, wrapping towels around themselves and huddling into them the way girls do. Hillary dropped her eyes, embarrassed. Thirteen, Joel thought. He hated thirteen.

Jamie tossed her towel onto a chair and cannon-balled into the deep end, splashing the black couple who stared at her, watched her swim under water then emerge in the middle of the pool. The diet-soda mom corralled the last of the soccer players out of the pool, and the good-looking mom finished her beer then rose slowly, following the others into the hallway. Joel turned back to the pool and caught Mary's eye. She had been watching him. Now, she looked away, taking a seat next to Jamie's towel, several feet from his chair. Hillary sat next to her mother and set her features on bored.

The pregnant woman grasped the little girl around her waist and propelled her through the water, the both of them laughing, the little girl straining to keep her head above the water. The woman looked at Joel, said, "'Bout time they left," and Joel, understanding she meant the soccer players, nodded.

"That's right," he said. "They were too rowdy."

The woman smiled and now Joel saw that she was younger than he had thought, that she wasn't that far from being a teenager herself, and he was sorry he had said *rowdy*. It was the kind of word an old man would use.

"I mean," he called out, "they were getting a little out of hand. For the younger set," he nodded at the little girl.

"Oh, her," she said, laughing, shaking her head, her long hair damp at the ends. "It don't bother her. Believe me."

Mary wouldn't look his way now. She stared at the water, watching Jamie dive down for underwater handstands. Hillary blinked, gazing across the pool at nothing. She said something to her mother that Joel couldn't hear.

"What was that, honey?" he asked. "What was it you said?"

But it was Mary who answered. "We're just watching Jamie swim," she said. Jamie twirled through the water, ejecting her stubby legs into the air. "That's all," Mary said. There was a touch of reproach in her words, and Joel remembered: *We can't cancel* this.

The black couple had slipped into the water and were swimming side-by-side, twin breast strokes. The woman put her feet down to stop, but the man kept swimming, more gracefully than Joel would have guessed. The pregnant teenager set her little girl on the side of the pool and leaned back, floating, her big belly rising from the water like a turtle. Jamie spun around and called to her mother and sister. "Come in," she said. "Swim with me."

"In a little while, sweets," Mary answered her.

"I'll swim with you, Jamie," Joel offered. He rose from his chair and stood at the edge of the pool. "How is it?" he asked the pregnant girl.

She grinned at him, not turning her head to answer her daughter who was whining to her, clearly tired. The black man with the well-groomed mustache swam back to his companion, rising up next to her and kissing her shoulder. Jamie waded to the ladder and pulled herself out of the water.

"It's nice," the pregnant girl told him. "Real nice."

"It's warm enough?"

"See for yourself," she said. The little girl sat on the edge of the pool and kicked furiously, splashing her mother.

"Joel."

It was Mary who spoke, but Joel turned to Hillary. She looked small and very young sitting there in the pool chair. It was the youngest she had looked since she actually was young, a little girl clomping through the living room in cowboy boots.

"I think I'll go on in," he said. He walked around the shallow end to the steps and lowered his foot onto the first step, the water rising halfway up his calf. "Warm," he said.

"I think it's heated," the pregnant girl said. "Are you on vacation?"

"Oh, no," he said. He descended the rest of the steps, cupping his hands in the water as he waded out, feeling the buoyancy of the water through his legs as he moved them. "It's my job. At the hospital. I do contract work."

"Oh." The girl smiled, relieved. "I thought that would be a hell of a shitty vacation." She laughed. *"Here."*

"Yes, this isn't exactly Hawaii." He watched the line of water against the girl's bathing suit, skimming the material across her belly, just under her breasts. He drew close to Jamie who darted under the water. "This is hardly the Bahamas," he said. The girl smiled, tilting her head a little and Joel had a flash of what she might look like without her bathing suit. He remembered from his wife's pregnancies the way a woman's body softened and swelled, allowing for new life. He imagined the girl's breasts, heavy and full, the blue veins etched across her immense belly.

"We're just here for a little getaway." The pregnant girl bounced her daughter on her knee beneath the water. The little girl screeched, falling back, then clung to her mother's arms. "Daddy will be home soon," she said to the child who lunged forward, grasping her mother's neck. The pregnant girl turned back to Joel. "He's in Iraq," she said, and Joel nodded, still straining to touch Jamie. He reached down and caught her ankle before she could swim away.

"Look what I caught," he called to Mary and Hillary. He pulled Jamie from the pool and set her, laughing, onto his shoulders. "Just look what I found." He tickled the bottoms of her feet and she flung herself backwards, into the water. Hillary again said something to Mary who nodded, said something back, and then looked squarely at him. She shook her head in a small, almost imperceptible movement, and Joel wondered if they'd been talking about him, what they had said.

"How long has he been gone?" This came from Mary at the side of the pool. She was looking past Joel at the pregnant girl. Hillary sat up a little, listening.

"Six months," she said. "He won't be home for a long time yet."

"Must be tough on you, on your little girl," Mary said. Hillary stiffened in her lounge chair, pulling her knees closer to her chest. The pregnant girl removed her daughter's hands from her arm and reattached them to her neck. She began to swim with her little girl trailing behind. "When's your baby due?" Mary asked, but the pregnant girl didn't hear her, kept swimming. On the other end of the pool, the black couple kissed.

Joel had seen the high school boy who'd caused his daughter trouble just once. The family had gone to one of the football games and Hillary surprised them by not sitting with her friends. She wanted to be with Joel and Mary. Going for hot chocolate at the concessions stand, Joel and Hillary passed a knot of boys. One stepped forward, calling Hillary's name. He ducked back into the group when he saw she was with her father, but not before Joel caught the smirk on the boy's face, that terrible knowing grin.

"I don't feel like swimming," Hillary said. "I don't feel like anything."

"Come on." Joel went to her side of the pool and rested his elbows on the edge. She hadn't let him go back to the boy and refused to tell even Mary what had happened. It's big, whatever it is, Mary had said. This is something very bad, she said.

"Hillary," he said. "I'm your father."

"No," she answered. "I'm not getting in. You can't make me. You can't make me do anything." She finally looked at him. Her eyes were shiny and angry. She had once been such a small thing, a tiny baby in the crook of his arm. He saw in her eyes the slim chance of his righting things. The pregnant girl set her daughter on the edge of the pool and put her arms out to catch her. Hillary had been born nine weeks early, small and uneasy with the world from the first.

"Joel," Mary said after a moment. "We're going up to the room. The girls are tired." She stood and walked to the edge of the pool where she waited for Jamie to climb out, handing her a towel.

Hillary had begun to cry, turning her face away from Joel. The pregnant girl rose from the pool and gathered her little girl in a towel. The black couple had climbed out of the water and were sitting again with their feet dipped at the side, talking. Joel took the steps out and stood close to Hillary's chair, water dripping onto the concrete around his feet. He looked down at his oldest daughter and held his hand out to her. She kept crying, her face turned away from him.

"Come on, Hillary." Mary bent to rub Jamie's arms with the towel. "It's all right. Everything is okay. We can come back tomorrow. Joel, we have the whole day tomorrow. Let her go."

But Joel kept his hand out to Hillary who pushed it away,

standing up. "No, thank you," she said. Joel wished he had done it anyway. He should have gone back for that kid and kicked the shit out of him for looking at his daughter like that, for whatever else Hillary wouldn't tell. Now, before he knew what he was doing, Joel swooped Hillary up in his arms. She struggled; he held onto her. "No, daddy," she said, but he began swinging her in the direction of the pool, counting. "One…two…" Mary called for him to stop; Jamie whooped and clapped. Joel heard the pregnant girl laugh. The black couple was silent; Joel didn't know if they were watching or not. Here was Hillary, in his arms. There was a time when she was even tinier than the squirming preemie, a tiny speck on the ultrasound screen, a girl in the making. Mary gasped. Joel loved his wife; he needed her. He loved his children. There were things he wanted to tell them; he wanted to keep them safe. "Daddy, let go," Hillary pleaded. "Please Daddy, let go of me." She closed her eyes, and Joel called out the last number, "three," swinging her out over the pool. He let go. There was the instant of his daughter hanging in the air, her yellow hair whipped up behind her, her limbs out, falling. Jamie and Mary held silent, unbelieving. Joel sucked his breath in and watched his daughter, frozen in that nano-second above the pool, holding onto nothing.

# The Core of Planet Earth

"Tell me about the Finneys," my father says. He has been sleeping on my couch for the past six months, since my mother passed away, and we have fallen into the habit of rising early to meet in my living room, talking through the gray hours.

"All those children," I say, remembering.

"Yes," my father answers, nodding. "What else?"

The Finneys were a mother and a father and a tumbling litter of children who lived next door to us when I was little. The children played in the woods behind our houses. At different times in the day, their mother appeared at the back door in blue jeans or sometimes in just a nightgown, calling the children home. They made great loops around the yard, running like mad, most of them, while others—the smallest of the girls—twirled about like pieces of dandelion fluff, their arms flung out, making slow progress to the door.

"They were wild," I tell my father. "Boundless."

My own mother, who wore long, loose skirts and chunky-knit cardigans, explained to me that the Finneys were evangelical Christians—such groups spawned prodigiously. From my hiding spots around the house, behind the hydrangea bushes, under the porch, behind the tool shed that housed our ancient push mower, I watched the children play and believed myself invisible. If they saw me—which they almost always did—I turned tail and ran so fast, so hard, I imagined it was fast enough, that all they could see was my disappearing smoke.

My mother read books and certain important elements of the newspaper to me. At dinner, she discussed scientific ideas and political principles. My father was usually sympathetic to her views, but when she found fault with our pious-minded neighbors, he often defended them. *They believe in literal truth*, she complained, waving away the abstract air. *How can truth*, my father questioned her, *be anything other than literal?*

They discussed further. My mother believed truth to be a malleable substance, different for how you look at it, for geography, for culture, for the season and the light and the year. My father had begun to see it instead as a fixed point, a reality that is only marred by a person's sentimentality. And, here, they argued over the nature of sentimentality, which my father believed to be an irrational dependence on a treasured perspective, *any* perspective. Belief in God, my father argued, was not inherently sentimental, just like science was not strictly free from sentiment. My mother refused to see it this way. Religion was a hallucination. Sentimentality was how you got there.

A librarian in a podunk, nothing town, my mother would never call herself a true intellectual, though she aspired to intellectual ways. She was also a minimalist and could not see the point to all those Finney children. Mrs. Finney was a mystery to her, and though she disliked the woman, she found she could not stay away. There came a day when my mother crossed the lawn and knocked on our neighbor's front door.

"No," my father says. "They came to us."

"That's not all," I insist. "*She* went there. Once."

Mrs. Finney and her husband, a tall, broad-shouldered man with a paunchy, weathered face, visited evenings, Bibles in hand, to discuss matters of life and redemption with my parents in our living room. I was supposed to be in bed, but I could not resist sitting at the top of the stairs in my pajamas to hear them. The Finneys spoke in quiet, reasonable tones about the will of God and the atoning sacrifice of Jesus' blood.

My parents said little in return, but I went to bed many nights wondering at what the Finneys were saying. I began to wonder if it was true that a person could have Jesus for a friend, if God was really everywhere, as the Finneys claimed He was. I listened for Him in the dark. My mother despised those God-talks, and though I never told her of my own spiritual ponderings, she brought down books, showed me pictures of dinosaurs and fossils of extinct birds and dog-like creatures caught in prehistoric mud. She turned to the stars. There once lived a scientist named Galileo, she told me, who knew the earth revolved around the sun and not the other way around; the Christians hated him for knowing it.

My father is clearly surprised to learn my mother sought our neighbors out on her own, if only once. He smoothes scraps of hair across the top of his head and frowns at me, puzzled.

"I don't remember her doing that," he says.

"She did. It was Christmastime, and she brought them a loaf of pumpkin bread. Mrs. Finney invited us in, and she and Mom had coffee in the kitchen." I shrug. "I went to play with the other kids." This is the hole in my story, for of course, I can't tell him about the conversation between my mother and Mrs. Finney at their kitchen table—I can't remember a thing I didn't live. But, I do recall the look on my mother's face when I left her there, a look I could not name until years later, one I have most often seen on my own children's faces. It was a glimmer of helplessness, washed away in a second by her cool repose—she held herself so carefully, especially in front of others—and I am unable to guess if she was questioning what might become of me, going off to run around with such scattered, wild children, or if she was more worried about herself, marooned there with Mrs. Finney. When I left them at the table, she leaned close to my mother and spoke quietly, my mother's fingers playing with the corners of a paper napkin on the table.

"The children took me to the little girls' room. The boys kept barging in to shoot us. They had these plastic guns." We weren't there for long. My mother came to retrieve me from the girls' room, and at the time, I thought it was because of the guns. It's only now that I wonder if she even knew about them.

We are quiet now as I search out something more, as my father studies me. Often, during our remembering, we come to these blocks of silence and don't try to move them. We sit staring them down until they move or melt away on their own. Today, though, I don't want to stay here with my mother taking me back inside, her starting up Shubert on the record-player, bringing out coffee, taking down a history book. I don't want to think of how tight and quiet our house felt, closed up against our neighbors.

"She didn't like the Finneys," I say, a means of conclusion, though my father keeps looking at me, unsatisfied. The house is still and cool, effused with the smell of rich coffee from the kitchen and autumn cold from outside. Soon, my husband will be up, I'll have to get the children out of bed, get them dressed.

My father says, "I always knew there was something about the Finneys. Something she struggled with."

I suppose he's right, but I can't give him everything. There are bits I'll hold back, just to look at them, just to see what's lying here in my hands, to think on what she might not have wanted him to know.

"When she took me to see Richard Combs," I tell him on a different morning, putting the words between us like a thought we're sharing in the same head, "I could tell she was in love with him."

He nods, as if he already knows this, or at least my perception of it. So much of what we're striving for is a creative act, this re-remembering. We must proceed carefully, and take our coffee quietly in the first cold light of the day, search out the connections, think on the things neither of us knows.

Richard Combs, my mother's favorite author, wrote of a boy who possessed in high order the one cognitive quality my mother lacked: imagination. The thin, hard-backed books stored on the highest shelf of my bedroom bookcase, away from my grubby hands, were filled up with stories of a young farm boy named Hank. Sparsely sketched in simple black ink illustrations, Hank was a scratchy little boy with holes in his britches and a spriggy hairdo. My mother liked to read the entire page with the picture turned to her chest before she showed me, for the surprise of it. The words were all in Hank's head, and they spoke of his launching space ships into orbit, or massive sailing vessels to sea, while in the picture, it was revealed that the space ship was nothing but a cardboard box, the ship only an old washtub. My mother read the stories with flourish, her eyes snapping with the cleverness of them. Each time she turned the picture to me, I feigned surprise and delight, though I often wondered what was so special about it, just a boy and a tree stump, or a boy with a clothesline imagined to be connected like the string of a kite, to the moon. Hank flew the moon on the end of a string, but I listened for the whoops of the evangelical children playing out back.

The particular attraction of the Hank books was not revealed until we were packed up for a day in Asheville. In the car, my mother told me, *Today, we will meet a famous writer.* She drove on, me glimpsing outside all the cars that passed. *Have I never told you, Therese?* my mother asked, laying a hand on mine, *Richard Combs was once just a boy from Carson. We grew up together.*

The problem was I was seven years old and only paid mind to what interested me. There was no reason for me to care much about meeting the man who had written these books I only liked a little bit, though my mother's enthusiasm intrigued me. We chugged up the winding narrow roads, rising out of our valley, and I stared hard out the window, looking the long ways down the mountain when we came to the outside of it, glimpsing out far into the glaring sun—I was still young enough to imagine that staring into it could turn me blind. I must have at least glanced at my mother, though, because I have a memory of her sitting there, squinting through her enormous sunglasses, her hair, starting to gray, gathered into a loose knot at the nape of her neck. When I return to it now, I try to look more closely, but I can only remember the details I attended to then, and my child-self did not know to touch her arm, to make her turn so that I could check her expression, measure the lines in her forehead.

"She looked miserable," I say, "but happy, too."

My father sets his coffee down and puts one finger to his lip, thinking. I continue.

The signing was harmless enough, held in a bookstore in the old part of town, full of cobble-stoned walkways and vegan restaurants. The shop was small and cluttered, and the man sitting behind the table was boxy and broad-shouldered. He seemed too large for his surroundings, me rising on tiptoes to spot him sitting at his signing table beyond the five or six middle-aged women, a few like my mother, with a child held to their sides, keeping a crooked line, their slim Hank books at the ready.

I turned shy when it was our turn. My mother stood smiling down at this enormous man and set a stack of books—one copy of each Hank book in existence—in front of him. *To Therese, my daughter*, she said, laying a hand on my head, both as claim and as a means of clamping me down—I was twisting away from her—*and to Monica. That's me.*

Richard Combs glanced up at us, smiling mildly, and opened the first book. He lifted a black pen to write. My mother, whose tenseness I could feel in her grip on my shoulder, said, *Richard*.

The man looked up at her, and his eyes turned from questioning—almost alarmed—to pleased. Richard Combs grinned.

*Monica Troy*, he said, and my mother smiled back at him, releasing my shoulder at last. I stayed, though, waiting for her to correct him; Monica Hodgins, I listened for her to say, but she just looked at him and waited for him to say more. *Monica*, the man said.

My father, hearing, only nods. Here is another moment for us to settle into the memory, to let the holding spots of my mother's life take shape, to pull taut the string we fix from that point to this one, mapping out my mother's constellation. I don't offer up the rest, how Richard and my mother bantered for a bit on their hometown, how she went into great detail, how much she loved Hank, what she was doing these days, her work at the library, her work raising me. I do not tell my father of how Richard Combs' eyes, after a moment, flitted to the growing line of dowdy women behind us, of the smile that stuck on my mother's face, how she nodded awkwardly, gathered her signed books and left the store with them still under her arm, having forgotten to pay. We stood outside the shop for a long time, her deciding whether to return, me yanking her this way and that, wanting a bathroom, a soda, to go romping through the shops. And how, in the car, I cried, begging her to return, to pay. I didn't fully realize the crisis my mother was encountering, and I couldn't imagine why those little books and that big, boring-looking man held so much importance to her.

My father doesn't know when I abandoned her, that I left her that very afternoon to knock on the Finney's front door, or that I know which part *he's* leaving out, for I somehow, in the years since, have pieced it together: the day my mother accidentally shoplifted occurred near the time my father did as my mother did, as I did—he went over to see the Finneys on his own. I heard him leave after I was put to bed. He returned late, and it wasn't long after that that he accepted the Finneys' invitation to visit their church. That was when the substance of truth was no longer debated at our house—it had become too important.

What's sitting between us now is all of this, and I find I cannot go that extra step, to show my mother humiliated in the book store. It's enough to think on how my mother was the only one who went to the Finneys' house and returned, unchanged. What I see now, though, in her truth-debates, in her going to our neighbors' house, even in her going to see Richard Combs, whose books were only about things believed, but not seen, is that she *wanted* to. What my father and I can't quite come to is what held her back, why she couldn't believe, and how our crossing over hurt her.

The first of my betrayals came moments after we returned, when my mother decided there wasn't enough time left in the school day to warrant a return, and I was left on my own while she went upstairs to her bedroom and closed the door. I listened to the unsteady quiet of the clock in the dining room ticking seconds from the twelve to the three and then took one of the signed Hank books from the pile she had left on the kitchen table.

The children weren't home from school yet, but the mother received me in a quilted house coat and, with a questioning look that melted into pity, took me into the house. We sat at the kitchen table and Mrs. Finney looked over my shoulder at the illustrations as I read aloud of one of Hank's journeys into his backyard. He drilled a hole to the mineral core of planet earth. It was Richard Combs' most scientific work, full of factual asides about the seat of magnetism and its place in keeping our planet in orbit. Here, Hank was uncharacteristically thoughtful, wondering if he himself grew heavier as he drew nearer the earth's central source of gravity.

When the children came in, the first to invite me to play was one of the dandelion puff girls. Finishing her snack, she dusted her hands off and clattered across the room, over the jumbled limbs of her brothers and sisters who were gathered round the table to restore themselves with punch and cookies, the room full of their talk and the sounds of their plastic cups being set on and lifted off the table, set again. The others had hardly noticed me, just one peering through the smudged lens of his glasses to study me. *Your name is Therese*, he told me. The others glanced over, then resumed their talk.

Reaching me, the little girl laughed before she made contact, before she extended her hand and tapped my arm. *I got you!* she sang out, screeching away through the back door, into the woods, me rushing up from behind to catch her.

# Love Falling

Eric knocked, three heavy thuds, and we stood waiting at the door, shivering. Small white houses lined the street behind us, each with a neatly shoveled walkway leading to a lighted front door, most with at least one crumbling snowman on its lawn. The cold, thin air was wet with falling snow. I kept my hands deep inside my coat pockets and stood still, not leaning into Eric as I might have had I been in a better mood, or less tired, or more enamored with his grosser-than-gross jokes, which he had been laying on over the past day and a half, straight up from Alabama.

"You're going to love it here," he said.

"If you say so," I answered and watched my breath disappear into the porch light. I stood stretching my legs and huddling into my coat against the cold.

The door opened and a tiny woman in a green pantsuit ushered us into the house, patting Eric's back and smiling. She looked my way as we dropped our bags and shed our coats in the hallway.

"Andy said you were bringing a girl," she said, giving Eric a sort of encouraging smile, and he introduced us: this was his aunt Gladys; this was his girlfriend, he winked at me, Julie.

"Julie!" She grabbed my hands. "Your fingers are ice, poor thing!"

Eric led the way to the den where I chose a seat on the couch. He sat next to me and Gladys, after hanging our coats in the hall closet, positioned herself across from us on the ottoman. When she blinked, her artificial eyelashes tangled like broken spider legs. Around us, the house was warm and tidy with vacuum marks in the mustard-green carpet and a neat stack of *Life* magazines like a miniature skyscraper on the coffee table.

She beamed at Eric. "Where have you been hiding yourself, mister?"

He leaned back and recapped the last ten years of his life, from his dropping out of school and leaving Wisconsin, for good, he said, to the year he spent in Canada avoiding the draft, to life since then, the months in New York, in Baltimore, in Ohio where he met me—he paused to squeeze my arm—and finally Alabama, where we'd been living with his brother and his brother's wife since September.

"I'm not cut out for construction work," Eric said. "Not much of a salesman either." He kept his eyes hooked on Gladys's until she gave a short laugh and looked away. Eric was blond, with green eyes, and a faded scar that ran from his cheek to his ear on the left side of his long, thin face. Chicago, he had promised me, would be our town. He said he could just feel it, all the good things in store for us here.

"Went door-to-door for a while, selling encyclopedias." He shrugged. "Not as glamorous as it sounds."

I stared at a grouping of mushroom needle-points on the wall and waited for Eric to tell how he'd also failed as a factory hand in Birmingham. But he was done talking, glancing quickly at me, then at Gladys, smirking a little though I couldn't tell what he was laughing at.

"I thought I'd fix beef Bourguignon for dinner," Gladys said. She frowned at her empty hands, laid palm-up in her lap. Eric caught my eye and winked at me. "I wanted to make beef Bourguignon for dinner tonight, but I couldn't make sense of the recipe. I put a roast in the oven instead." She looked up, her smile dropping away. "The roast," she gasped. She looked at me. "I forgot the roast."

She sprang up and clattered into the kitchen. From around the corner, I could see her bending to yank a pan out of the oven. The smell of burned meat wafted into the living room.

Eric put out a hand to stop me when I stood up, gesturing to me to stay put. He'd told me about his uncle's wife Gladys, about her losing a baby to crib death when she and Andy first married, about a fling she'd had a few years ago with a neighborhood boy just returning from Vietnam, among the last soldiers to come home. Before any of that, she was a small-town beauty queen. Her talent had been twirling batons, and for her grand finale, she threw her baton so high, it struck one of the lighting fixtures in the high school gymnasium where the pageant was held. The fixture flickered, then went out, and no one saw Gladys catch the baton and finish her routine.

"I'll go," Eric said, but just as he started to move towards the kitchen, there was the sound of a key in the door. It opened and a man—Andy, I guessed—stepped inside. Slipping out of his coat, he looked first at me, then at Eric standing immobile between the sofa and the kitchen.

"Eric," he said, nodding. "Nice to see you."

They shook hands. Andy was a large, boxy man with a thick-jowled, ruddy face. He was obviously much older than Gladys, though it was difficult to pin down Gladys's age since she wore such thick makeup, and because she was as small and fidgety as a child.

Andy turned to me. "You must be Eric's girl."

I nodded. "I must be."

He raised his eyebrows, glancing at Eric, but said nothing. A thud came from the kitchen: Gladys dumping the roast into the trash. Andy's face turned grim as he moved to the kitchen. "It's ruined," we heard her tell Andy. There were the choked sounds of her sobbing, then the scrape of shoes on the linoleum, and the sobs became muffled. Eric and I stood silently next to each other, watching the kitchen.

"That woman's crazy," Eric said, giving a low whistle.

Andy and Gladys came out a moment later. He held her at his side, her arms dangling, her face murky from smeared mascara. She smiled weakly as Andy announced, "Dinner will be ready momentarily." He squeezed Gladys's shoulders, crushing her closer to his side. "Hope you like TV dinners," he added, laughing a small, hollow laugh.

Andy left for the city after breakfast the next morning and Eric went out to catch a bus into Wheaton. Andy hadn't been able to land him a job at the radio station where he worked as Eric had hoped, but he had a friend who managed a shoe store in a new shopping mall thirty miles away. His friend had agreed to give Eric a shot as a salesclerk. "Pays more anyway," Andy said, and though Eric agreed, I saw the muscles in his jaw tighten. He left for the bus stop without a word and Gladys, still wearing her nightgown, rose to clear the breakfast dishes.

"Looks like it's just us girls," she said. "We'll have a chance to chat."

She went to the sink and began to fill it with dishwater. "It's snowing again." She frowned, looking out the window over the sink. "What will we do with all this snow? The Whitmans, our neighbors, say this is nothing. They're from northern Minnesota. He sells insurance, she goes door to door, Avon calling." Gladys looked out the window at the snow as she washed the juice glasses, handing them to me one at a time to dry and put away in the cabinet. I tried to picture her as a beauty queen, twirling her baton on an unlit stage. She slid the frying pan, with feathered bits of yellow egg, into the water.

"You can almost see their house from here," she said, pointing.

After dishes, Gladys set about the housework, cleaning the

floors, dusting the shelves, accepting only bits of help from me. My mother had never been one for housework, and I could imagine what she would think of Gladys and her lemon disinfectant, her starch, her mushroom needle-points. She would say, *that's a fine thing to run away to, Julie.* My father had left us when I was seven. Maybe because of his leaving, my mother and I were very close, but during the past summer, something had broken between us. I was spending my days at the lake, sunbathing and meeting up with Eric—mystery boy then—and I was only home for dinner. She pulled on her cigarette, giving me long, studied looks over her cold macaroni and cheese, exhaling the smoke through her teeth, her parted lips. She said, "Who is he? Who is this guy who thinks he can have you?" It was just the three of us, and my little brother sometimes laid his fork next to his plate and looked down, into his hands, embarrassed to be a boy.

Gladys rested during the afternoon while I looked through her cookbooks. I found the recipe for beef Bourguignon and studied the steps, thinking I could save Gladys from another burnt roast. Since Eric had taken the bus to Wheaton, I drove our car, which was actually my car, a 1965 Datsun I had waited tables after school five nights a week to pay for. The street Andy and Gladys lived on was icy, and the car's steering felt a little off, too stiff, but the highway had been plowed, the steering wheel turned with difficulty, and I drove to the A&P. Along the way, I passed a restaurant, the Halfway Diner, and a couple of gas stations. I paid for the groceries with money Gladys had given me and returned to their house to cook dinner. When I arrived, she was bathing, the entire house touched by the sweet scents of her body oils. By the time dinner was ready, she was dressed in a yellow mini skirt and matching jacket, her face made-up, her short, dark hair elaborately styled. She sat in front of the television in the living room, watching *Phil Donahue.*

She said, "Julie, you're a dear."

We sat down to eat when Andy came home, slipping his coat

off at the door. He grinned at me over the platter of meat, the steaming bowl of peas, the basket of warm rolls.

"Magnificent," he said.

By the time Eric came home, we'd finished dinner. I started to fix a plate for him, but he said not to, that he was too tired to eat. Later, when we were alone, he told me, "It was so damn boring." He passed his hands over his face and rubbed his eyes. "What I can't figure out," he said, "is why I always end up with the shit job. Why does it always happen to me?" I told him about the trouble with the car and he sighed, said I just didn't know how to drive it. He reached for me then, kissing me. I kissed him back, my hands on his shoulders, pressing my body against his. I couldn't get close enough to him, far enough away from myself, from this house, from Gladys. I thought of her and that neighbor boy, how it must have been between them. Gladys did everything with a deliberate slowness, the sponge making long, thorough swishes across the linoleum as she mopped the floor on her knees, and I pushed my palms up Eric's bare chest, then spread them out, over his shoulders. I kissed him long and hard, and when he lifted my nightgown to touch me, I kept my hand on his, guiding him. He caught my rhythm and we moved slowly against each other, each movement a measure of restraint, holding back until it was painful, until we couldn't breathe and there were no thoughts, until we were hollowed out and spent on each other.

Afterwards, I lay in the dark and imagined the snow falling outside. I watched it in my mind in the same way Gladys had watched it through her kitchen window, admiring its blankness, how white and empty and cold it was. I watched it fall from the sky like fluffs of nothing, filling the roof over us, covering the streets.

"What's grosser than gross?"

Eric asked us this at dinner a few nights later. I had made chicken cordon bleu from some chicken breasts in the freezer. Gladys dropped a pale, thin hand to her lap. It was just the three of us since Andy had taken some clients out for dinner and wouldn't be home until late.

"What's grosser than gross?" Eric asked again, giving me a little nudge under the table. He was still in his work clothes, his shirt wrinkled, his nametag pinned to his collar. Gladys looked up, blinking, opening her eyes wide to unstick her lashes.

"What's grosser than gross?" Eric persisted.

Gladys sat staring at Eric, unsure of what to say. Her eyes flicked towards the door and I knew she was thinking of Andy, wishing him home. She finally asked, "What?"

"Jumping off a building and snagging your eyelid on a nail," he answered, grinning and picking up his fork. He held it suspended over his food.

Gladys smiled uneasily and I waited for Eric to start eating. He set his fork down, though, still looking at Gladys, and I could see him working himself up. He licked his lips and spoke again.

"What's grosser than gross?"

This time, she glanced at me before answering. "I don't know." She spoke in a small voice and touched her napkin, twisting it in her hands. She pressed her lips together and braced herself for the answer.

"Eric," I started. "Eric, please." He ignored me, keeping his eyes on Gladys's.

"Eating a bowl of cornflakes," he whispered, leaning towards her, "then finding out your brother has lost his scab collection." He wasn't smiling anymore. His neck and face were flushed and I could see the tiny white line across his cheek. Gladys sat pale and silent. I laid my hand on his leg under the table, hoping to calm him, to make him stop. He and Gladys were in a separate place, sealed off from me.

Eric shifted his weight in his chair and my hand dropped away. He whispered, "What's grosser than gross?"

She slowly raised her eyes to meet his.

71

"Eating rice off a plate and watching the rest fly away."

Gladys nodded and, when Eric finally looked away, his eyes wild, she went back to taking tiny bites of food. Eric finally began to eat his chicken cordon bleu. He ate quickly, then pushed away from the table, saying he would go out and see what the hell was wrong with the car.

"Julie won't stop talking about it," he said.

We watched him leave; then Gladys rose to clear the dishes. I tried to apologize for him, but Gladys waved it away. Eric stayed outside for more than an hour, then returned and sat on the couch without speaking, staring at the blank television screen until Gladys rose to switch it on.

Later, when Andy came home, Gladys met him at the door, slipping her arms under his coat and around him, him bringing his arms around her, looking at us over her head. They stood that way for a long moment, just holding each other. Finally, Gladys moved away, towards their bedroom, and Andy narrowed his eyes at Eric.

"What happened here tonight? You say something to her?" Andy's face was flushed. "You did, didn't you?" He made a move towards Eric and seemed about to say something else, but then he stopped, shook his head and glared again at him. "You just mind your manners, you understand?" Eric said nothing and after a moment, Andy turned and followed his wife down the hallway, still in his coat.

Eric quit his job at the shoe store a few days later. He said, "The manager hates me."

Andy shook his head. "That wasn't your job to lose." He looked at Eric for a long moment before he picked up his briefcase, moving towards the door. He stopped, turned, and said, "Just to remind you, this is not a permanent arrangement, your staying here. Just you remember that."

It had stopped snowing, and Gladys watched the windows, guessing when it might start again. Eric hadn't bothered her since the night of the grosser-than-gross jokes, but I saw him watching her from a brooding distance, and I couldn't figure out why he hated her. Gladys acted as though nothing had happened. Sometimes, she came into the kitchen and peered into my pots and pans, opening the oven to squint at the ham, the pot roast. She said, "Maybe I'll make chicken and dumplings tomorrow night," but she never did. I started doing more of the housework, and most days, she sat at the kitchen table, drinking coffee until her hands shook.

At first, I said nothing to Eric about his quitting his job. That night, he didn't eat dinner at all but only came inside to change his clothes, then was back out in the snow again. He said he was going to see about fixing the car. Through the kitchen window, I saw him sitting on the curb and smoking. I wanted to go to him, to sit down next to him and breathe in the cold air together. I thought it could be like the summer, the two of us lying at the end of the fishing pier at the lake, looking up into the dark sky. I stood at the sink and thought of this, watching him, but didn't go.

When he finally came in, hours later, I was sitting at the kitchen table with only the light from the range on. Gladys and Andy were in bed.

"You waiting up?" he asked. "What's a matter? Couldn't go to bed without me?"

"You promised we'd be getting our own place," I said. Something had changed in me when I saw him standing there in the dark kitchen, leaning against the counter I'd wiped down after dinner. "That means making money," I said, and he glared at me. "I can't stay in this house anymore, Eric. You don't know what it's like to be cooped up in here everyday. To be stuck with *her.*" Every moment I spent watching Gladys stare blankly at the wall or the top of the kitchen table or a television screen was a moment closer to insanity.

"The three of you are making me crazy," I said.

"Fuck you," he said, quietly. He had never talked that way to me, and I sat there, absorbing his words, the rush of them beating into my fingertips.

"My mother was right about you," I told him. My hands were shaking.

"Shit, Julie," he said, laughing, "I could have told you that."

I stood, raising a hand to slap him, but he grabbed my shoulders and twirled me around. He put his arms around my waist, pinning down my arms, and pressed the side of his face against mine. "Julie," he whispered. "It's okay. Only a minor setback," he promised me. "Okay?" I said nothing, but I felt my body relax into his. He kissed me. "I'll fix it. I promise." I finally relented and followed him to the pull-out sofa. I expected him to reach for me, but he rolled onto his side with his back towards me. I lay in the dark with my eyes open to the tiny spots of light that slid across the ceiling with passing cars. I thought that I could be in any of them, floating away.

He went out in the morning to buy a paper and then settled at the kitchen table with Gladys, drinking coffee, Gladys standing every once in a while to sweep the kitchen floor, or run the vacuum cleaner, to take clothes out of the dryer. I watched Eric study the want ads, frowning over them, circling a few with a pencil nub I'd found in the kitchen drawer. After a while, he rose from the table, stretching, and went into the living room to watch television with Gladys. When I asked, he said there were some possibilities, a few places to call, but he wanted to look again tomorrow. "Don't worry," he said, glancing up at me from the television. Gladys turned to smile at me. Then they were two staring heads, each facing the screen, motionless.

Eric joined Gladys again at the kitchen table the next morning, drinking coffee and reading the paper while I started washing the breakfast dishes. Gladys took up a section of the newspaper, and, after a while, Eric put his pencil down. They read every part of the newspaper, even the business section and the real estate pages. They were mostly quiet, but sometimes they spoke, discussing the news, a sale at Penney's, the obituary of a 46-year-old used-car salesman who left behind no family, only cats. I stood in the doorway, watching them until he turned back to the want-ads, picking up the same worn pencil from the day before.

"That neighbor boy," he told me when Gladys stepped out to get the mail, "you know, the one she screwed? Well, he was an asshole. I met him once. You wouldn't believe what an asshole he was." He shook his head, as if that was the only tragedy here, the boy's being an asshole.

"You were here before? Just a few years ago?"

"They were sneaking around," he said. "I *helped* them, I lied to Andy." He folded his arms across his chest. "It was before I met you, before you got your chance to piss off your mother. It was back before any of that, Julie."

"You helped them?"

It started snowing that afternoon. I found myself pausing, dust rag in hand, to look out the picture window in the living room, out across the lawn, dusted with the snow, falling on the grass, the tree stump, not yet sticking to the sidewalk or the street. I stood watching for a long moment, thinking I could stand here long enough to see all the grass covered in white, and maybe it would begin to stick to the road. Gladys and Eric were on the couch, watching television, and I turned to them.

"Look," I said, "snow."

Neither seemed to hear me at first. Gladys kept her eyes on the television screen, but Eric was looking at her, watching her watch the television. After a long moment, he turned to me and we were still, just looking at each other. Something passed between us then, some understanding of why he watched Gladys, of why he hated her. I stood staring at him, coming to this understanding, his hand there on the couch curved in the direction of her thigh but not touching. He saw me looking at his hand and brought it to his lap, turning his eyes away from mine. Finally, Gladys spoke.

"I just love this part," she said.

I took the bus out and put in an application at the Halfway Diner the next afternoon. The waitress behind the counter was a large woman with wiry black hair. There were no openings at the time, she said, but she would keep my application handy, just in case. I thanked her and turned to leave, but she stopped me. "Hey," she said. "You want a cup of coffee? It's cold as hell out there. You might as well have a cup of coffee." She took her glasses off, letting them fall on their gold chain against her ample breasts. I said I couldn't stay and thanked her again. She nodded, said she would hold onto my application, and warned me to be careful driving. "It's awful out there," she said. From the restaurant, I walked to the A&P for steaks. Andy's and Gladys's neighbors, the Whitmans, were coming for dinner.

Gladys was ironing a tablecloth in her bathrobe when I returned. Eric wasn't there and Gladys shook her head when I asked her where he was. "I forgot to iron the tablecloth," she said. "How could I have forgotten the tablecloth?" She moved the iron quickly, jerking the cord with each hasty swipe across the fabric, and rested it to dab at her eyes with the sleeves of her bathrobe. "He should never let me have people over. He just shouldn't *do* this to me."

"Stop," I said, taking the iron from her hands. "Go. Get dressed."

"You're a doll," she said. "An absolute gem."

She was in the bedroom when Andy and the dinner guests arrived home together. Andy took their coats and introduced us. "This is our nephew's friend," he explained. "Julie, meet Howard, his wife Florence." I smiled and nodded while Andy fixed drinks. "Where's Gladys?" he asked. When I explained that she was still getting dressed, Andy joked that he should have guessed. Howard laughed, slapping Andy's back. He was a slight, black-haired man with deflated red cheeks and hard blue eyes. Florence, a tall, loud-voiced woman, waved the men's laughter away.

"Let her primp," she said, winking at me. "We girls have our ways."

Andy sat with the Whitmans in the living room while I finished dinner in the kitchen. I turned the heat down under the steaks, then dressed the salad and took the cheese puffs from the oven. Bringing out a platter, I saw that the Whitmans were seated on the couch, with Andy perched next to them on the edge of his easy chair. Eric had appeared and was kneeling at the fireplace, poking at the logs. Gladys stood behind him, watching him work.

"We plan to call her Wendy," Howard was saying, lifting a glass of scotch to his lips. "Florence wanted to name her." Florence leaned over to explain they were adopting a baby from Vietnam.

Andy nodded. "It's a good thing you people are doing."

Eric rose from the fireplace, dusting off his hands. A few small flames bobbed among the logs. "Let there be fire," he said.

"The babies," Gladys said. "I've always wanted a baby," she said. Howard looked up sharply, then turned away. Florence coughed into her hand. "But I wouldn't want one from *there*," Gladys continued. "I wouldn't know what to do with a baby that wasn't really mine." She smiled up at us. "I've always wanted one of my own." Her fingers played with a piece of hair that had fallen in her eyes.

"Sure you do," Eric said. "Neighbor boy couldn't even give you that much." Gladys blinked back at him, confused. "So good of you people," Eric said, turning to the Whitmans, "to adopt one of *those* babies."

"Now, you listen here," Howard started, but Andy raised a hand to stop him.

"You son of a bitch," Andy said evenly, clenching and unclenching his fists at his sides. "You useless son of a bitch."

"Oh, dinner!" Gladys caught her breath. She turned to Andy. "Please, let's have our dinner. Andy, please." Nobody moved. "Julie? Florence? Let's finish up." Gladys lifted her hands, fluttering her fingers as if she meant to gather us into the air.

I turned to glance back at Eric as the three of us filed out of the room. He stood staring into the fire. Andy kept a few feet back, muttering to Howard who nodded, looked at Eric, nodded again.

In the kitchen, Gladys yanked the lids off the pots on the stove and declared everything finished. Florence held back a little. She caught my eye as I turned from Eric. She said, "Quite a boyfriend you have there." I said nothing, only turned to the stove, getting the food ready for the table. "Real classy," she said. I felt her watching me as I dished the beans into a serving dish and moved the steaks onto a platter.

Later, I went to sit next to Eric outside on the curb. I touched the thin scar on his face and waited to see what he would say to me. After a long moment of us just sitting next to each other in the freezing cold, I reached for his hand. He lightly squeezed my fingers, then pulled away.

I left late that night, when the house was completely dark and quiet. The snow was slicked over with a thick crust of ice and new snow was falling cleanly through the cold air. There were a couple of inches on my car and ice crystals on the windows. The street lights cast yellow globes of light against the black sky. I set out to walk since the buses didn't run at night.

Using change from my coat pocket, I dialed my mother's number at the pay phone next to the diner. I cried at the relief in her voice. She said, "Hold tight, Julie." After I hung up, I went inside the restaurant and sat down in a booth next to a window to wait out the few hours it would take her to drive up. There were a few men sitting at the counter, smoking cigarettes and drinking coffee. They called out jokes to the waitress, a different one from this afternoon. She was younger, with blonde hair and red lipstick. "Keep your shirts on, boys," she said. "I'll be with you in a minute."

She smiled at me. "What can I get you, honey?"

I ordered a cup of coffee. When she brought it to me, I held the mug between my hands and let its warmth spread through my cold palms, up my fingers.

# Birds of Illinois

Maud began having sex dreams about the retarded bag boy at the start of April. She woke to gray pressing against the window, a light, even rain falling on the muddy grass outside, no mercy in sight. In her dream, the retarded boy's open, dull grin loomed above her.

She rose, finally, and drew the blinds closed against the clouds, pulling her robe on and stepping out of the bedroom. Her husband Donald, who always woke early, was already in the kitchen burning breakfast. He had retired from the telephone company last Christmas and now, with spring approaching, Maud found him standing at the sink watching the rain through the window. He had planned to spend his retirement working full-time in the yard and was aggravated by the soggy weather.

"Morning," Maud said, approaching.

He startled, turning from the window. "Morning yourself," he answered, slipping his hands into his sweatpants pockets as he used to do in his suit and tie, a composure he quickly assumed when someone caught him alone and preoccupied. Maud was ashamed of her dream, unable to stop thinking of it, but she maneuvered easily past her husband, reaching for a mug in the cupboard in a natural movement, calm. It was a talent she had developed early in their marriage, the ability to converse on daily matters while her mind skipped far away. Donald never guessed anything beyond what she said, and he rarely gave question to what she was thinking. Maud's sister Nancy, whose own husband was anything but pleasant, once observed that Donald was a most agreeable bastard.

"Been like this all week," he commented, as if Maud had just arrived from far away and didn't know the local weather conditions. There was nothing but corn and soybean out there beyond the grass and the other houses—rows and rows of ordered agriculture, bent only for the horizon deep against the turn of sky. Donald's job for the past thirty-four years had been to plan out the system of telephone wires across the endless farmland, and sometimes Maud pictured him stringing them along the poles like threading so many tall, wooden needles, him swinging from pole to pole like a trapeze artist. She imagined him working this way though she knew he rarely went out with the work crew, that most of his tasks were completed at a desk, him penciling in his calculations over computer-drawn blue lines—tidy work.

Maud murmured acknowledgement—stubborn weather—and poured herself a cup of Donald's too-strong coffee, then took a seat at the table. The foggy visions from her dream stayed with her so that even as she sat there, sipping, Donald giving her the space and quiet she needed to fully awaken, she was thinking of the bag boy, a young man named Tyler who, in reality, was somewhere in his twenties, his having bagged groceries past his teenage years. She called him retarded though she wasn't completely certain on that count—there was something very simpleton about a boy so desperate to please, all those smiles and alert attention to his bagging. She could not get over the surprise of the dream, not just its scandalous content, but also its insistence, its realness, compared with this, sitting down to gritty coffee, the bacon still cooking, black, while Donald returned to the window.

"It would be nice," Maud said, "if the rain let up by next

weekend." Janie, their daughter, and their sons, with their families, were coming home for Easter. "For the egg hunt," she said.

Donald nodded, not yet turning away from the window. "I expect they'll come, rain or shine." Then, after a moment, he said, "I'll be going into town this morning, to Harold's." This was the town's hardware store, little more than a couple of aisles of nails and washers arranged in coffee tins, a variety of screwdrivers. "I can stop by Star's," he offered, and for a moment, Maud pictured it: Donald shuffling along the aisles, trying to distinguish between cans of French-cut green beans and the standard variety, finally choosing the wrong thing and then carrying it and a package of chocolate-covered peanuts to the checkout. He'd nod glibly at Tyler, having no idea just what feats this boy was capable of in his wife's imagination, and smile at the checkout girl, a divorcee in her forties who always gave a little wink to her male customers, even the babies.

Donald was looking at her now, waiting. Outside, the rain dripped from the eaves.

"No, thank you," Maud answered. "We'll get by."

Nodding, he drew his hands from his pockets, readying for departure. He took a sip of his coffee, then examined the oily contents of his mug before emptying it into the sink. He pointed to the backyard. "Look," he said, "a cardinal." Maud followed his gaze; there in the bare sycamore was a spot of bright red, flown away almost as soon as Maud glimpsed it. "What a beautiful creature," Donald noted, and Maud pictured him again hanging from his telephone poles, pointing out the birdlife against a clear, blue sky, gazing down on the fields so far below him. Marveling again at the bird's impressive beauty, he turned off the burner under the destroyed bacon and left, walking back into the bedroom to dress while Maud pulled herself upright and stepped across the slick linoleum to the stove. She took the pan to the sink and filled it with sudsy water, not caring that it was still hot and the bottom would warp. It was the third frying pan Donald had ruined in his retirement.

81

Though she had promised herself she would wait until her usual shopping day to go to Star's, by noon, Donald had not yet returned and Maud found herself putting on lipstick at the bathroom mirror. She pinched her cheeks, a cosmetic ritual from her girlhood, one that still worked—somewhat—to restore color to her features, some trick at inspiring blood flow. The bag boy, she thought ruefully, was another trick.

Star Grocery's parking lot, just a side alley of maybe thirty spaces, was not even half full. Maud, parking her Toyota and checking her makeup once more in the rearview mirror, felt foolish and old. She gathered her purse and made sure to lock the doors, a habit instilled by Donald who held caution in the highest importance, even in tiny Brinkley.

The air inside the store was bright and cool, easy listening music piped in. Maud raised her hand to wave at a harried mother with small children clinging to her—one of Maud's neighbors—at the checkout, and Tyler, lifting a plastic bag with a family-sized box of sugar cereal bulging out the top, turned to smile at her, a slack-jawed grin, his head cocked to the side. He was tall with bushy dark hair, broad shoulders, and long arms that seemed somewhat loosely attached to his body. Maud nodded at him, struggling to free a cart, and he returned to his bagging, her watching the back of his neck, thick and red with a v of dark, course hairs. Maud had always been careful to trim away that excess when cutting her own boys' hair years ago. She remembered it—setting one of them down on the stool in the kitchen, towel draped around his neck. She snipped and chatted, the boys twitchy from the word go. Now, Maud wondered who cut this bag boy's hair, if he lived on his own or was cared for yet, some mother or aunt her own age, someone she would most likely recognize, distantly, as someone she'd gone to high school with, maybe a year or two older, more likely younger. Despite herself, she caught a glimpse of her dream, and, thinking of it, it was really more of a sensation than anything she saw, and not even that—a sense of closeness rather than the actual feel of him. He was a large person in real life, awkward and deliberate, but in her dream, he was more than that—he filled the entire room.

Maud hastily set about her shopping, going first for the green beans, then collecting various other goods, antacids and oatmeal, a box of graham crackers, a bag of jelly beans from an Easter candy display, a package of ground beef. She exchanged hellos with the rooster-headed butcher, a man she had known since high school, one she had never much liked for reasons so old she no longer remembered them, and picked up a package of margarine and cottage cheese, a pitiful winter tomato. It was nothing she could make a meal of, but now, it seemed a disastrously odd endeavor to come shopping on a Tuesday. She hurried with her selections, saying hello to the checkout girl, nodding again at Tyler who, spreading open a plastic shopping bag, tossed in her loaf of white bread and pronounced, "Bread." He gave a short laugh, and pointed, "Jelly beans. That would make one heck of a sandwich." As he spoke, his Adam's apple bobbed in his thick, trunk-like neck. He leaned closer and she stared at his blunt white teeth, his pink gums. "A candy sandwich."

She gave a tiny nod. "What's this?" he asked, peering closely at the bottle of fruit-flavored Tums. "Hey, I get it. You'll need it after the candy sandwich." He glanced up at her, waiting for her to acknowledge his small joke. She murmured yes, she always took Tums with everything and he gave her a funny look. "O-kay," he said, and shook his head, amused.

Maud touched her cheeks; her face felt warm. She was unable to stop herself from remembering again the feel of him from her dreams, in scattered flashes, as she watched Tyler scoop up the tiny produce bag of tomatoes and let it slide down his palm into a grocery bag. He stacked her cans of green beans, her peanut butter, and Maud watched his fingers work, the intent look on his face, his mouth open a little in his concentration. She felt a prickle run up her spine as she caught sight of his lips, a little chapped, full.

"You like this rain?" he asked. Maud nodded, said she supposed it was good for them, that they needed it. She wrote a check and handed it to the check-out lady who punched at the register, giving little notice to Tyler. He shook his hair out of his eyes as he loaded the last of the plastic bags into Maud's cart. "Yeah," he answered. "We have to have rain. People don't like it, but we can't go too long without it." He grinned at her, his lips curling back, and it was this gesture, this simple earnestness that brought Maud back to the opinion that while he may not be full-out retarded, he displayed a sort of childishness that didn't match his ruddy features. Here was a young man, twenty-something and large, talking to her with the same easy excitement her children used to bounce about in, their happiness spilling endlessly out of them. This boy seemed to enjoy her attention; Maud imagined he wouldn't mind if she stood there chatting with him at the check-out for the rest of the day.

Having finished, he clasped his hands behind his back and stretched. He asked, "You need help with these?"

Maud hesitated; he always offered but she'd never accepted before. Yet, today, she found herself answering yes, that would be so nice, and again felt ridiculous, following his broad person out in the drizzle, his lugging her few bags. Tyler strode straight to her Toyota, and Maud felt a tiny thrill at this—he knew which car was hers. She hurried ahead to open the trunk. He loaded the groceries, then turned back to Maud, giving her another sloppy, blunt grin, and a salute, good-bye. Once more, she sensed the bigger-than-life dream of him, and before she could stop herself, she reached out and touched his wet arm. She felt the curls of hair beneath her fingers, the clench of muscle, the warmth of skin. He pulled back, his simple, stupid face set in gaping confusion, and he turned back to the store, an odd little smile lighting across his face. Maud leaned against her car, watching him walk under the light sprinkle of spring rain, a flock of blackbirds scattering across the sky above Tyler's head.

As she drove the narrow streets of downtown, passing the shops, the high school, the baseball field, before she turned onto her road, she thought of cutting the bag boy's hair, maybe even shaving his face at her kitchen sink. She imagined the thick, white shaving cream and the scraping away, the smooth, soft cheek below. In this picture, she was young, wearing a pressed salmon-colored dress, one she remembered from years ago when the children were small and clamoring at her knees. No matter the years that had gone by, Maud yet recalled how it felt to carry each of her babies, the places within her, the tumble of budding arms and legs and feet against her insides, between the bones of her rib cage. The launch began those years ago, at the impatient shifting inside her, a sensation Donald didn't know a thing about. Once home, Maud parked her car in the driveway and sat for a long moment, wishing so desperately for sunshine her teeth ached.

Over the next few days, the dreams continued. They grew murky, full of dark, foggy purples and blues and greens, as if the action was happening deep in the ocean, distant beads of light swelling from above. She woke Saturday morning so caught up in the hazy dimensions of her sleep that she hardly recognized her surroundings.

Donald had risen early and taken off to the lumber yard to pick up supplies for some new project Maud didn't want to think too much about, and she was slow to rise, resting in bed far longer than she usually did. Later, when the phone rang, she was jerked back to her real life by the sound of her daughter's voice.

"Janie," Maud said into the telephone, "I was just thinking of you. I'm getting all ready for the weekend. Tell me, when does your flight arrive? Do you know it yet?"

"Listen, Mom, that's why I was calling."

Maud's heart sank. "You're still coming, aren't you? You and Alan?" Over Christmas, Janie had brought home a boyfriend from Boston, a fellow law student in gray wool slacks, tiny wire glasses perched on his long, thin nose, and Maud had not warmed to him as Donald had. She watched as the boy listened to Donald speak of the birds of Illinois with a mildly amused expression on his face, the way one listens to a child, raising his eyebrows in mock interest when Donald went into the flight patterns of the golden finches, the feeding habits of hummingbirds.

"Oh, yes. Yes, we're still coming." Janie hesitated. Maud realized she had been holding her breath, hoping Alan wouldn't come, wishing he and her daughter had parted ways, and now she exhaled, waiting for Janie to say more. "It's just that we have some news to share." She paused. "Big news. We want to come a day or two early and spend some time with just you and Dad. Is that all right?"

"Of course," Maud said, the idea of what her daughter's *big news* might be closing like a vise around her chest. "We'll be happy to have you."

"Oh, and Mom," Janie went on, "I'm sure you can guess about this, about what Alan and I have to tell you, but I wish you wouldn't. I just want to tell you in person. For you to be surprised." She sounded so hopeful.

Maud laughed. "Sure, honey. I can be surprised. I can be anything." For a moment, she was in the ocean with Tyler again, the water filling her ears and turning her movements slow and weighty. Four days. Maud had four days to muster up a plausible replica of happy surprise. She told Janie good-bye and went for a cold wash cloth to press against her forehead while she rested on the sofa. The house felt small and overused.

Blessedly, today, she had somewhere to go. The community college in Hoopeston offered continuing education classes on Saturday afternoons, and over the past couple of years, Maud had attended sessions on Japanese pottery and Appalachian candle-dipping. Last summer, she had begun her memoir. This spring, the class was on Russian cuisine and was taught by a tiny pixie girl in her mid-thirties with short-cropped, greasy hair and close-set green eyes nearly hidden beneath thickly mascaraed lashes. Her name was Olga, and she was born in St. Petersburg back when it was still Leningrad; she told how the old women who sold tickets in the train station refused to call the city by any other name. Maud wondered what those old women, the *babushkas,* thought about young girls like Olga moving to America to teach blini-making. During breaks, Maud watched Olga lean into the counter at the snack bar in the student union, smoking her foreign, sage-scented cigarettes, terrorizing the college boys with her sexy-haughty gazes. But Olga's husband—Maud had seen him just once—was only a pale-faced Midwesterner, a Caterpillar man from Peoria who now taught auto mechanics at the high school. To Maud, though, his homeliness only intensified the mystery surrounding Olga, her traveling so far just to marry a pasty farm boy. Maud's sister Nancy, who begrudgingly allowed Maud to register her for these classes, spoke of the primitive, scythe-wielding life still lived by post-Soviet Russians. "It's a lovely little convenience called a green card," she said.

When Nancy came to pick her up for class, Maud was still fretting over Janie's impending announcement. She stepped into Nancy's Plymouth and fastened her seatbelt, thinking, *marriage.* Despite herself, her thoughts snagged on the bag boy, his light fingers on her skin, the new, briny sort of buoyancy of her dreams. She closed her eyes and tried to clear her mind, but the hazy images had become a constant presence, a sort of haunting, and Maud felt Nancy squinting at her, wondering.

"What are you grinning about?" she asked, taking her cigarette from her mouth, a long, thin stream of smoke escaping her pursed lips. The farmland passed, tilled and ready but not yet planted and Donald's system of crisscrossed telephone wires floated above.

"It has to do with sex," Maud told her. "Sex and *me.*"

"Oh, yeah?" Nancy asked, interested, then laughed. "What's Donald asking for?"

"It's not that," Maud said. The mention of Donald made her

stop. She thought of him sawing away in the garage, of the mess of lumber and nails he was creating, what Janie's Boston boy would think of the effort. "It's not anything," she sighed.

"What is it? What have *you* been asking for?"

Nancy laughed out loud, her smoker's gravel dragging along. Maud took a long, choking breath and finally Nancy realized she was upset. She leaned over to touch her sister's arm.

"Maud?" she tried. "I'm sorry." She pulled onto the shoulder and stopped the car. "Honey? What is it? What's the matter?"

Maud pictured the retarded boy leaning over her, felt his hands on her body. She thought of Donald coming home with his arms full of lumber, taking a serious look at things from the perspective of his frayed flannel shirt, happy in his retirement.

She couldn't speak, and after a moment, she heard Nancy rifling around in her purse. There was the scratch of her lighter catching and then quiet, a few cars drifting by, the sky thick with clouds that Maud imagined were made of steel, unimpressionable. She wouldn't tell Nancy after all, not even that small relief. She sniffed and looked long out the window, the plowed dirt stretching out wide and empty before her.

"I'm sorry," she finally said, turning to face Nancy who regarded her suspiciously, still waiting to find out what the problem was, and finally, Maud begged her to keep driving. During class, Maud felt Nancy watching her, snatching glances at her while Olga explained how to roll out the dough for palmeni. She explained the elasticity of the dough, how to work the pockets open, how to poke the ground mutton inside.

After class, Maud suggested a late lunch. "Or, how about an early dinner," she said as they left campus, "Whatever you want to call it."

They ate a meal of thick, grilled sandwiches at a coffee shop, and then, Maud asked Nancy if she had time to do some shopping. She sought out shoes, dresses, flatware, a new frying pan. They lingered over the shops at the mall, then slowly pushed a shopping cart through the aisles of an enormous linens store. They stopped for coffee and perused the aisle of a book store. Maud purchased a book of Chinese poetry, and Nancy squinted at the title on a novel, flipped through the pages, asked her again if she was feeling all right.

Later, as they were driving home, Maud said, "Janie is bringing that Boston boyfriend home with her," and Nancy talked the rest of the way, telling Maud how she ought to handle him, what she ought to say to him.

It was nearly nine o'clock when Nancy left Maud at the front of her darkened house, but it felt much later, midnight at least. She sucked in the crisp air, the rain gone but leaving an autumn-like chill, the dark smell of far-off livestock and feed, and stood before her house, shopping bags in hand. She made no motion to enter the house, and after a moment, Donald appeared, walking briskly across the drive, asking her, in a gentle, perplexed way, if she was okay, claiming she'd given him the fright of his life. Maud allowed him to guide her to the house, but answered only that she needed to do some shopping and she was sorry she hadn't called. She noticed a splash of bright pink paint—pink!—on his cheek, and saw that his hair was disheveled from his figuring with a pencil on a board, him pushing his fingers through, thinking. There was the woodsy scent of sawdust about his flannel shoulders.

Maud said, "Well, the house is still here," and Donald gave her a confused look, then one of relief, understanding. He brought her in to see what he'd started in the garage. "Birdhouses," he said. "Half a dozen of them." Though he hadn't gotten much further than cutting the pieces and splashing a bit of paint on the board to test the color, she caught a glimpse of what he envisioned, those miniature cottages with their whistling, happy birds, blue jays and cardinals, maybe robins, flying in and out, building their nests, setting about the instinctual task of keeping house.

On Monday, Donald mentioned they were out of lunch meat. There were no more pickles in the jar, only a lone Pepsi in the refrigerator. Even the loaf of bread Maud had picked up just a few days earlier was nearly gone since she hadn't prepared a decent meal all week, just sandwiches and Donald's cheese toast. When the children were still at home, Maud planned out the family meals carefully, balancing vegetables and breads and always one glorious meat dish: a meatloaf or a roast or a fried steak. She had taught Janie how to cook—the two of them in the kitchen, cleaning this, cutting that, checking the oven, always this way. They did this even when Janie was a teenager and continuously performed her own disappearing act, there in the flesh, gone in spirit, and Maud was thankful for the cooking, for the collected hours of standing side by side, working towards a common goal: dinner.

After breakfast, Maud sat down to make a list. Besides the usual staples and a cut of roast, she added ground mutton and onions to her list. Cabbage. Fresh mushrooms—she'd have to consult her notes to locate the kind Olga had insisted on for gold mushroom soup. Sour cream, too, since Russians added a dollop of sour cream to everything. Olga had told the class this, speaking in her severe accent that had taken weeks for Maud to grow accustomed to. Since then, she had grown so used to the accent that as she made the list, she heard Olga speak the ingredients in her ear: *There is no compromising when it comes to mushrooms for the soup and mutton for the palmeni.* The boys were coming Saturday and would be home for Easter dinner: ham, potatoes, macaroni salad. Janie was coming with her boyfriend a day earlier and Maud thought it would be nice to serve a Russian meal.

"We're having palmeni when Janie arrives," Maud told Donald when he came in from the garage. He nodded though Maud knew he had no idea what palmeni was. She hesitated. "What do you think," she asked, "of this boyfriend?"

Donald stood by the sink in his work jeans, filling a glass with tap water. Of course, she and Donald had discussed the boy before, months ago when he visited with Janie, the awkward look of this boy, all dark and skinny. Maud remembered a shrug from Donald, a comment on the boy's grasp of contract law, how he'd seen a combine in disrepair on some farmer's back lot and called it a corn crib. Donald had been this way with the children since they'd reached adulthood, shrugging and complacent, just happy to let them be. On the day each left, Maud saw his shoulders droop. It was a part of the general winding down of their lives, the way his body relaxed at seeing each leave and Maud hated him a little, watching.

"Alan?" he asked, holding his glass to his lips. She nodded impatiently, laying her pen down to look up at him. For once, she would fully wait for an answer, insist on a fully stated opinion from her husband. "I just meant," he continued, "you didn't say his name. It's Alan."

She crossed her arms. "Yes," she said, "Alan. She said she had news. *Big* news."

The rain had stopped near the end of last week and Donald had spent the weekend walking the backyard, squishing through the wet grass, coming in to comment to Maud on how long he thought it would take the soil to dry adequately, where he planned to plant the clematis, how it would grow to cover the posts on the birdhouses, what variety of birds he thought their yard would likely attract, what sort of wildflowers to plant to bring in the butterflies, which species loved the Midwest. Donald watched through the window now. Maud thought he was trying to spot a meadowlark pecking through the wet ground for a rain-loosened worm.

"I think he's smart, just like our Janie." He glanced at her, then looked back to the backyard. "You know," he continued, "none of them have ever chosen exactly what we've wanted for them. They have their own ideas about the way the world works." He took a long swallow and poured the rest of his water into the sink. "Janie more than the others. But she's always been right. Law school, the rest. It all works for her." He sighed, stretching, and Maud pictured the boy in his polished shoes, his dark sweater-vest, his neatly pressed dress-pants. He must have hatched on a city train, wearing those kinds of clothes.

"We can get goldfinches and cardinals if we put out sunflowers," Donald said, clearly finished with the talk about Janie and her news. "They might come," Donald said, "if we put out hulled sunflower seeds."

Maud wanted to go to Star's alone, but Donald had something to pick up at the hardware store and reasoned they could drive to town together. She would do her shopping while he poked around Harold's, and then, he could help her get the groceries into the car. Fine, Maud agreed. She only wanted the time inside the store, alone in the bright aisles, completing her tasks, to bask in her efficiency and spy on the bag boy when he wasn't looking, hoping he wouldn't remember the scene in the parking lot, if he even thought of it in those terms. Probably not.

When Donald dropped her off, Tyler was sitting out front on the bench, taking his break. He was talking to one of the checkout girls, a heavy girl wearing the sort of low-slung khaki pants that only accentuated her pudgy figure, made worse by the tight-fitting nylon *Stars Grocery* golf shirt. Yet she was pretty, in an overly made-up, back-alley sort of way that Maud noticed had become popular, and Tyler was talking to her, giving her those sort of goofy laughs that these young girls, Maud had seen, had so little patience for. Yet, this girl was smiling back. She still looked vaguely put-off, the prerogative of the young being constant boredom, but she seemed to be doing more than tolerating Tyler. Maud walked by, watching, but neither looked back at her.

In her dreams, she saw less and less of Tyler. Visuals of any kind had been washed away by the turbid dream-sea, and the last few nights there had been nothing to see, and nothing to hear. Only touch. They had become sea creatures with slick skin and unwieldy bodies, thumping against each other, and yet strangely amorphous, one pouring into the other. It was hardly about sex anymore, yet it held its carnal pleasures, the slick sucking of water-soaked skin flapping against each other, twirling around in some dark space, something like water, something like endless space. Maud did not perceive the other person there to be Tyler by any physical signs; she couldn't see him and they were no longer murmuring to each other. Still, it was him, a knowledge as close to Maud as the sound of her own name. Upon waking, Maud half-existed in that swirling state, her waking to the same blue gauzy curtains that had been there for half, maybe more, of her marriage, her own bedroom having an ancient, distant feel, as if she were only waking to another dream.

And now, in her normal life, Donald was across the street at the hardware store, talking weather with the other old men, probably, rainfall for the month and obituaries, and here was Tyler, just coming in from his break. Maud glimpsed him smiling to himself, in love with that girl, all synthetic fabrics and fat. She pushed her cart down the grocery aisle, thinking: flour, eggs, meat.

In the refrigerated meat cases in the back, Maud searched the cellophaned packages. Olga had said ground mutton was the best for the palmeni filling, that in Russia, each kitchen was equipped with a meat grinder, and that it was best to grind the meat yourself, mix in a raw egg, cut the onions so fine they sting your hands, and add them with the mutton—one half kilo. Olga rolled her eyes. One pound, she explained.

There was only ground beef in the case, that and one single pound of ground pork, and Maud considered buying both, mixing them, figuring it was the best that could be done in a town as small as Brinkley, as American and heartland and beef-eating a place to be found anywhere on the globe. She touched the package, the pink meat squishing beneath the plastic, then changed her mind. The picture came to her: she and Janie in the kitchen, her explaining that only ground mutton could be used, Janie raising her eyebrows at that, nodding. Boston boy was in the back, nibbling a rolled blini dipped in whipped sour cream.

Maud motioned for the butcher behind the counter.

"Mrs. Holman," he said, smiling. If he had seen her at church or a high school football game he would have called her Maud. She'd known Charlie Briggs since grade school, back when he was a skinny boy with an awkward gap between his front teeth. The gap remained, but his shoulders had thickened and his round belly pushed against his apron. He stood grinning at her, stooped over his chopping block, a good distance back so as not to disturb the shopper with the presence of raw animal flesh. Maud wondered if there was real blood back there, if he drained it in the sink. Just how raw was the meat that came to Charlie Briggs?

"What can I get for you today? The family coming to town? Those boys still eating good?"

Maud smiled, leaning against the case. "Yes, everyone's fine." She hesitated. "Charlie, I need two pounds of ground mutton. I'll take a few chicken breasts as well. Maybe," she thought, deciding, "a few pork chops." Yes, she would cook this week. She would cook until she could hardly stand and here would come Janie and her boyfriend into a house that smelled of savory foods. At the front of the store, she glimpsed the checkout girl leafing through a magazine, and Tyler coming through the automatic glass doors with a few shopping carts wrangled from the parking lot.

Charlie Briggs looked at her. The whites of his eyes were yellowish, aged along with the rest of him. His screaming red hair had faded to rust. Maud remembered something about him from high school: Charlie was slow to learn in every subject—even gym class gave him trouble. Now, he stood looking at Maud, finally repeating her, "Mutton? You say ground mutton?"

Maud nodded. She had made up her mind. If a thing could be found in Soviet Russia, even post-Soviet Russia, whatever small changes that had brought in the availability of sheep meat, well, then, that same thing ought to be available here in Brinkley, Illinois. "Yes," she answered. "I'm making a Russian dish. *Palmeni;,*" she pronounced the word carefully. "Sometimes, it's translated as meat pies, but really, that's making it sound larger than what it is." Maud thought. "Meat pillows, maybe. Meat-filled clouds." She shrugged. "I'll need ground mutton. Or ground veal. Tell me," she said, squinting close, "do you have any veal back there?" Charlie put his pencil behind his ear and came around the partition, wiping his hands on his apron. He seemed larger as he came, larger and slower, moving something like how Maud imagined a buffalo would swagger. He glanced quickly at her and turned away, as if he were looking for help.

"Now," he said, standing next to her at the meat case, spreading his hands to indicate the variety. "We have your ground chuck, ground beef. Round steak. Roasts. Any of these to your liking?" He squinted at her.

"I'm sure you've never had palmeni before," Maud said. "It really must have *just* the right sort of ingredients, you see?" She glanced at the front of the store. Tyler was nowhere to be seen though the checkout girl, the one he had fallen in love with today, looked up from her magazine. Maud realized she was raising her voice. "My daughter is coming into town," she said, trying to lower her volume. "She'll be announcing her engagement, and we'll need a special meal."

Charlie slapped his hands together. "I've got it," he cried. "Let's ground the steak. You can't get much fancier than that." He chuckled to himself.

"No," Maud said, and to her embarrassment, she did feel the start of tears at the back of her eyes. "*No.*"

Tyler approached the back of the store, pushing a wide broom across the bright tile. He glanced at Maud who felt as frail as tissue paper, as one of Donald's birds, her standing there, pleading with the butcher, the retarded bag boy lopping along. She thought of her dreams. Why, they were ocean mammals, she realized. Something like whales or dolphins or some other sea creature with a yearning for contact, beings who swam free and strong. Maud held out her hands to the bag boy, remembering how she had touched his arm in the parking lot, and now tears came. She called to him, "Please, Tyler." She stepped towards him. "Please."

The boy stopped short, blinking. Maud took another step towards him. "Oh," she said, her face wet with tears, and she felt the reality of who she was, this old woman.

"Mrs. Holman," Charlie Briggs started, and already, Tyler had disappeared into the stock room. Escaped, Maud thought. "Let's just get our bearings here. All right?" The butcher looked around him and Maud cried into the palms of her hands. She tried to stop, to shore herself up, wipe her eyes and walk out the door, thinking she might just leave Brinkley forever. She wondered if Tyler was going after a chair for her to sit in, if he was glancing her way, concerned, and she knew that he was not. After a moment, she heard the slow, scuffling sounds of someone drawing near.

"Donald," Charlie Briggs said, his voice full of relief. "I'm afraid Maud is a little over-tired." The butcher chuckled, desperately uncomfortable. Here came her husband's hand on her back.

"What is it?" he asked. "Maud, what's happened?"

"Ground mutton," the butcher said, whistling. Maud heard the mocking smile in his voice. Charlie Briggs had been the biggest fool in high school and now here he was, laughing at her.

Maud dabbed at her eyes with the tissue Donald had handed her and she wondered where it had come from. He was not the kind of man to carry tissues, and now, he had given her one and he was moving his hand, rubbing lightly across her back. The picture came to her of what Donald himself had looked like in high school, the person he had been, and she saw his calm, quiet manner, him sitting at the back of every classroom. She saw him stepping down the hallway, nodding politely at each pass. He was a neat dresser, with tidy, short-clipped hair. Donald had been voted most courteous. She thought of his birdhouses in the backyard, of how he had let the children go, of how he stood on the porch and looked back at their house and found something new to start each time.

She wondered if it was the same with her, if she ever seemed new to him, if there was anything more for them to do with each other.

"Your lady wants mutton," Charlie Briggs said again. "For a Russian pie."

"Then," Donald replied evenly, "we'll see about getting her some." He took her elbow and led her away from the meats, through the sugar and flour aisle, past the young checkout girl, out of the store. Donald moved on, helping Maud step across the asphalt parking lot, guiding her into the car. He turned the key and let the engine idle, taking her hand and holding it between both of his as if it were an achingly cold day, spring still months away.

"Let's get out of here," he said, and she nodded, resting her head on his shoulder. She put her hand to his chest, and through his flannel shirt, through his skin, his bones, unseen flesh, there was his heart, beating soundly. Maud sucked in her breath, surprised by the strength of that instrument, her own heart quickened by the solid warmth of his body. She shifted in her seat to move her hand up across his collar bone and around his neck, slipping her fingers into his collar and bringing her palm back down in front, across his bare chest. Leaning closer, she kissed his cheek, then pressed the side of her face against his.

# Springtime on Mars

I had only caught glimpses of Elise Stanley before that long ago cold spring morning when she stepped out of the crowd and into the circle of bystanders. She and her son Timothy, who was in the seventh grade with me, had just moved into the house at the end of the street, the last one before the railroad tracks. It was an old neighborhood with small brick houses shaded by giant oak trees. The trees' roots grew up against the sidewalk, leaving the concrete crumpled and broken in places, and during the winter, the tangled branches blocked the sun so that the snow, when it came, was slow to melt. Sometimes in the evenings, just before dinner, I watched her pass our house on her way home from her job at an attorney's office on the south end of the street. She walked in high heels, moving briskly down the sidewalk with a detached air about her that I admired. "She's divorced, Paige," Aunt Martha, my mother's sister told me. She raised her eyebrows significantly. "And she frequents the Blue Tavern, over in Kernersville." I was twelve then and didn't fully understand the real and imagined dangers my aunt, who considered herself more worldly than my somewhat provincial parents, was trying to warn me of. To me, Elise was already a sort of miracle, her walking down the slick, uneven sidewalk like it was nothing, not even looking down to watch her feet step over the ice.

Nathan Price, the boy to receive Elise Stanley's special kindness, was a sad case even before the accident. His father was a chemist at the insecticides plant near Burlington and his mother was a reclusive housewife who paid one of the Croswell boys to do her grocery shopping. She sent Nathan to school with cans of sardines and packets of crackers in his bag lunch; for dessert, he popped the lid off a mini-can of mandarin oranges. He ate by himself because he smelled. It wasn't just the sardine oil on his fingers, but also a sort of alkaline funk in his greasy hair, and a damp, mildewed scent on his catalogue-ordered golf shirts. Nathan was skinny, too, and he was smart in a dumb way, annoying the teachers with endless questions as to the precise location of Greenland, and whether or not our founding fathers would have insisted on free speech if they'd known about MTV. Nobody touched Nathan, not even bumping into him in the crowded hallways, not even to push him or sucker-punch him in the kickball line. The teachers also kept their distance, careful not to graze his shoulder when they leaned over his math problems. Nathan was worse than an outcast; he was a disease we were all doomed to catch.

He didn't try to talk to the other kids at school. His father dropped him off at the Friday night football games and Nathan sat close to the band section, then left before the last quarter was over. I never heard of him calling anyone on the phone; he didn't even go to church. The only time he tried to fit in was at our bus stop in the mornings. I think he felt safer in our small group: just me, the new kid Timothy, and my best friend Carla Phillips. At least, Carla was still *my* best friend; I wasn't sure if I was hers anymore. We had ended up in different homerooms this year and Carla had been making other friends, leaving me out more and more. Lately, she had started going to the mall on Saturday afternoons with Samantha King, a girl who everyone knew had started kissing boys in the woods beyond the railroad tracks when we were still in the fifth grade. Carla and I didn't talk on the phone in the evenings as we used to, and sometimes the twenty minutes we spent waiting for the bus together in the mornings was the only time we spoke all day. I was quiet by nature, though, and Timothy kept to himself, playing with green alien figurines in the grass, not seeming to notice or care how childish he looked. Occasionally, he glanced up to explain to us the terrific gravitational pull Jupiter demonstrated, keeping its sixteen moons in orbit, or how some scientists believed the universe was a breathing entity, slowly expanding, the planets and stars pushing out against each other until cosmic forces shifted and they would begin to draw close to each other again. "It's like this," Timothy said, demonstrating with his hands, cupping them close together then slowly separating them, fingers opening as his hands moved apart. It was hard to believe Timothy was the son of glamorous Elise.

Carla was the focus of Nathan's attention. On the morning of the accident, she sat on top of her school books with a compact mirror balanced on her knees while she applied mascara. She was not allowed to leave her house with make-up on. I was not yet interested in such things, but Aunt Martha, who was still single at thirty-five, didn't believe me. There was a womanly balance she was trying to press upon me—something between being too plain like my mother and being too garish like Elise Stanley. Aunt Martha passed me tubes of lip gloss on the sly and bragged to her friends that I was twelve going on twenty-three.

Nathan stood watching Carla, his hands in his jeans pockets. "You look good," he said, and she rolled her eyes. He turned to me. "Doesn't she?" he asked. I mumbled some word of agreement and caught Carla's eye. Timothy sat a ways back, burying a plastic green Martian in fallen cherry tree blossoms. The morning smelled of cold, and of toothpaste.

Nathan said, "I can walk on my hands."

We were used to such claims. He also said he could hold a lit match and recite "The Gettysburg Address" before the flame burned his fingers. He could read Braille; he could juggle. His father had bought him a car, a Volvo, before he could even walk. We never told him we didn't believe him, though it seemed to go without saying. Mostly, we did our best to ignore Nathan Price, wishing for the bus to hurry around the bend.

I didn't even glance his way. I asked Carla, "Did you study for the science test?"

Carla shrugged, not answering me, and screwed the top on her mascara. She zipped up her make-up bag and cocked her head, giving Nathan a lopsided squint. "I don't believe you," she said. Her eyes narrowed as she measured him up. "You can barely walk on your feet, you moron."

I stared at Carla. Even now, I'm not sure why she challenged him except that her father had just lost his job at the same insecticides plant where Nathan's father worked. This was the mid-eighties, when everything was a boom except in our town where the main businesses had been dwindling away. The bank and the department stores were gone; the plastics factory had closed down the year before. Now, the insecticides company had opened another plant overseas and slowly, layoff by layoff, our own plant was fading away. But we weren't thinking about these things that morning at the bus stop—Carla only knew her daddy had lost his job and Nathan's daddy hadn't.

"Do it," she said. "Walk on your hands."

Nathan didn't look like he was about to do anything. His face went pale and his eyes widened, bright with fear. I wanted Carla to leave him alone, but I didn't tell her to. Stepping back a little, I glanced at Timothy who had looked up from his toy to watch. I could see his alien more clearly now, a bulb-shaped green head attached to an impossibly small body, spindly arms and legs at its sides. The figure lay on the ground, Timothy's hand resting on it.

"There are some," he told us, "who believe spiders are alien life forms."

I suppose he meant to distract Nathan and Carla, but neither of them seemed to be listening. They were eyeing each other. Nathan gave Carla a grim little nod, deciding something. Dropping his backpack, he lifted his arms and began rotating them slowly backwards in sweeping circles, limbering up. He glanced once more at Carla before he leaned over, placing his hands on the asphalt. With a small grunt, he hefted his legs off the ground. His squeaky-white sneakers sprang to the air and then, just as quickly, they fell back again.

"I knew it," Carla said. "Maybe now you'll shut up for a change."

She folded her arms across her chest and watched for the bus. I searched her face to see if she had softened at all, if she would be difficult today, stubbornly quiet as she sometimes was these days. The morning was especially quiet and still, too cool for May, and it felt like spring would never come. Few cars passed us that morning, and it seemed we stood there longer than we ever had. I studied Carla's profile, wondering if she would give me that tired look across the lunch table later today, the look that told me she couldn't believe we were still friends. Nathan was standing in the road with his face flushed, frustrated because Carla had turned away. Timothy returned to his Martian. The bus was late.

"They crashed to earth on a meteorite billions of years ago. That explains our irrational fear of spiders. It's primal," Timothy explained, marching his alien through the grass.

The sun rose into the clearing across the way and I had to squint to see Nathan get on all fours again, kicking his legs up and balancing. He wavered a bit, then held steady, taking a few quick steps into the road. Hands on the asphalt, feet in the air, that horrible JCPenney shirt slipping down around his neck, the white skin of his stomach exposed to the cool air, he went. He was *doing* it. He moved in quick, jerking motions, the blood deep red in his face, his arms so skinny I half-expected them to break in two under the weight of his body. Though I didn't dare glimpse in Carla's direction, I felt the three of us taking in this sight, the phenomena of Nathan Price moving across the street on his hands, his arms shaking with the effort.

"Okay, okay," Carla huffed. She shoved her hands into her jeans pockets. "You did it. Now get out of the road, you stupid shit."

Nathan righted himself for a moment, shot us a grin, and got down on all fours again. He sprung his legs into the air.

"You're a dumb ass," Carla told him and went back to watching for the bus.

Nathan was halfway across the far side of the street when it finally arrived. It lumbered around the corner faster than usual, braking late, then coming between us and the sun just over the clearing. Even as the bus struck his body, I didn't understand what was happening. Here was Nathan in the last second of his handstand before he pitched over, the bus lurching to a stop over him. He lay half under the bus, half out, his body flat against the street.

The sky was bright and still and it seemed nothing bad had happened, that nothing bad could have happened. No one spoke; for a moment, nothing changed.

The bus driver was Davis Croswell, a senior at the high school. He wasn't the same Croswell boy who did Mrs. Price's grocery shopping for her—that was Joey—but all of the Croswell boys were alike in two ways: they were the first takers when it came to odd jobs, and they each had the easy draw and unhurried mannerisms of country boys. He swung out of the bus to check what he had hit; then, seeing, he stood motionless, his big hands hanging empty at his sides. The kids on the bus were rowdy as always, talking loudly and jumping in their seats. Some of them hung their heads out the windows to see what was going on, and one yelled, "What'd you hit, Davis?" Davis didn't answer them. He'd left the door open, and a few of the kids followed him off the bus. They were laughing at first, happy to be on the street on a Tuesday morning, not yet at school. Then they saw what had happened, smiles falling off their faces. Their eyes moved from the road to Davis to us, the bystanders. We were each frozen and silent, except Carla, who drew in big gasps of air and hugged her arms to her chest. Davis glanced up, catching my eye. For a moment, I was afraid he was going to ask me what to do.

"Is it him?" he asked. "Is that the Price kid?"

He didn't appear to be asking anyone in particular. He leaned over, clutching his sides as if he was going to be sick to his stomach, but he regained control of himself after a second and tapped one of the boys standing close to him.

"You," he said, "go call an ambulance." He pointed to the Phillips's house behind us, and the boy took off across the lawn. "Nathan?" Davis squatted next to the bus. "Nathan?"

I wanted to tell someone to move him. He seemed vulnerable lying there, only his legs and his feet showing, and I had a crazy thought that if we didn't move him, he would get hit again. Most of the other kids were off the bus now, standing in a semi-circle around the front of it, watching. One boy said, "He's crying." He bent down to peer under the bus. "He's crying," the boy said again. "He's awake and crying." Another boy said, "His whole body is broken." One of them whispered, "Is he dead?"

I looked back at Carla, her arms wrapped tightly around her. Timothy was up now, and I saw him slip something into his pocket, that green alien. He turned, as if he could feel me looking at him, but I shifted before our eyes could meet, before the knowledge of what had happened could pass between us. The cold air slipped in through my jacket collar. There was the smell of burnt diesel, the bus hovering. Davis Croswell stood with his hands on his hips, closing his eyes, then opening them, shaking his head and mumbling to himself so low we couldn't hear him.

After a moment, I became aware of some of the neighbors coming up behind us, everyone keeping quiet, only whispers and rustlings of hands in jacket pockets. Mrs. Croswell held her two youngest boys at her sides, her fingers over their eyes though they peeped through, each clamoring for her to pick him up. Mrs. Phillips, Carla's mother, came carrying a cordless telephone. She pressed close to Carla and rubbed her daughter's shoulder. She was crying, whispering, but Carla did nothing but stand there, her breathing finally easing off a little, slowing down. Mr. Phillips was there, wearing a pair of jeans and a white t-shirt. He kept himself a few feet away from his wife and daughter and asked an old man from the street over if he knew what had happened, if anyone had witnessed it. He kept looking at Carla as he spoke, and I knew he had guessed what had happened, and who had seen it. Others stopped their cars, strangers who knew nothing of our neighborhood, who didn't know Nathan Price or any of the rest of us, those who wished they'd taken a different route to work that morning. Mrs. Whitmire appeared on her porch in her robe, holding her hand to her mouth. Some of the men talked about moving the bus. They rubbed their chins and shrugged. Mrs. Croswell touched my arm. "Has anyone told Helen?" she asked. Helen was Mrs. Price's first name.

I didn't notice Elise right away, her slipping out of the crowd and into the circle. It was different to see her like this, in full light, the sun picking out red streaks in her dark hair. She wore black high heels and a purple suit, the skirt so short and so tight, she had to pull it up almost to around her waist and crawl on her elbows to get to Nathan. The semi-circle was silent, watching her disappear beneath the bus. Most were incredulous, not understanding what Elise Stanley was doing there, crawling on the asphalt, wondering if she was going to cause any trouble. I think there were those of us who expected her to perform CPR or some other life-saving measure, and we held our breaths for a miracle. I kept waiting for something supernatural to happen, for Nathan himself to crawl out from under the bus and shrug at us, embarrassed to have caused such a scene. I shivered in my denim jacket, the air chilled and bright. After a moment, there was a hand on my shoulder and my whispered name, "Paige." I knew without turning to see that it was my mother. She squeezed my shoulders, and together, we waited.

The men finally organized a means of moving the bus. Davis Croswell climbed back inside the driver's seat and shifted into neutral while the men gathered at the front and on the sides, grunting and pushing; one of the older men squatted and watched the tires move, telling Davis how to steer. Once the bus was rolled back, sunlight filled up that space and we saw Elise lying next to Nathan, who was splayed out on the street, his head twisted to one side. Elise's face was close to his and she was talking to him, too softly for any of us to hear. He was conscious, though fading, fresh tears on his cheeks, his eyes unblinking. She kissed his face and cried while Nathan's blood seeped into her blouse, her hands, and even, in the decades it took the ambulance to arrive, into her hair. She stroked his shoulder. I felt pulled away, watching her. Her tears wet his face.

The emergency workers moved Nathan's body to a stretcher, and from there, to the ambulance. Elise picked herself up and stumbled away, her face expressionless and pale beneath her make-up. She stood in the grass, apart from the rest of us, and no one, not even Timothy, went to her.

Helen Price arrived just as the ambulance was pulling away. I later learned that Mrs. Croswell had first rung her doorbell, then knocked and banged at her door, and finally had gone around the side of the house, peering through windows, still pulling along her two little boys. She came in through an unlocked door at the back and found Mrs. Price in the basement, folding towels.

Mrs. Whitmire took her in her Buick, and together, they followed the ambulance around the bend, towards the highway. We watched them go; then my mother wordlessly steered me back to our house. She guided me to the upstairs bathroom where she undressed me as water filled the tub. She helped me in, then began to soap my arms. My limbs were heavy, achy, and I was grateful for my mother's hand beneath the washcloth, for her fingers on my scalp, for the warmth of the water. She rinsed my hair with a plastic cup from the kitchen and helped me into my robe, then led me back down the stairs to the couch in the living room where we spent the rest of the morning watching talk shows.

Near lunchtime, Aunt Martha arrived, coming in through the back door, breathless from news of the accident. She rushed into the room, then stopped, seeing me and my mother there on the couch, the chatter from the television only noise. Her eyes slid over to my mother's then back to mine.

"You all right?" She stepped toward us. "Paige? Are you all right?"

I didn't answer, and she stood back as if she wasn't sure she should come forward, as if she suddenly was awkward in our house, a place she ate dinner at more nights than in her own apartment downtown. The phone rang, my mother jumping to answer it in the kitchen, and now my aunt came to me, reaching for my hand. I could hear my mother speaking quietly from the other room but I couldn't make out the words for the voices coming from the television set. Martha gripped my hand and though my face was turned away, I felt her eyes on me, searching.

After a few moments, my mother returned to the couch, clicking off the television on her way. Martha rose, stepping away, and my mother took her spot next to me, her hands folded in her lap. My mother was a musician, a pianist. Her fingers were long and white, and they always seemed to be doing something purposeful, something beautiful, even when they were folded quietly in her lap. She cleared her throat, sighed.

"I have some bad news." She hesitated. With the TV off, the house seemed more than silent, like time stopped. The sunlight fell in slats on the carpet through the windows. I watched my mother twist her wedding ring around her finger. Martha remained quiet, though I knew she was listening. "Nathan's heart failed before they could get him to surgery," my mother said. She touched my hand, leaning close.

I nodded but said nothing. Out of the corner of my eye, I saw my aunt give my mother a small, grim smile before she stepped back into the hallway, then out the door.

Later, I told my mother, "It was Carla's fault." The afternoon was drawing dark, just before my father was due home from work. My voice was gravelly from not talking. "She dared him to walk across the road on his hands. She egged him on. She *made* him do it."

My mother watched me for a moment before she shook her head. "No, Paige," she said. "That's not right. You know it isn't right. There's no reason this happened." She left me then, hurrying to the kitchen where I glimpsed her standing by the counter with her face dropped into her hands. She returned to me with wet eyes and sat very close. She was determined to get me through this.

"I know why this happened," I whispered, and she pretended not to hear me.

The next evening I went with my parents to the visitation at the funeral home. People came out in great numbers and formed a long line from the closed casket where Mr. and Mrs. Price shook hands and smiled dimly at the guests. There was an unbreakable hush in the crowded room, the adults standing stiffly in their slacks and button-downs, the kids hanging close, and it wasn't just because there'd been a death or because it had been a young, tragic death. We stood in the plush room, our shoes sinking into the carpet, and watched the door. Everybody was waiting for the same thing, but Elise never came.

Many of my classmates were crying though I don't think any of us truly understood why we cried, all of us experiencing a vague sort of guilt, an uncomfortable feeling that we didn't belong here, grieving Nathan Price, and yet, we couldn't stay away. There was something particular about me and Carla, the only eyewitnesses besides Timothy, and I caught the other kids sneaking quick glances at me, jerking their eyes away when I met their gaze. Already, a rumor had started that Carla had pushed Nathan into the street. I didn't hear anyone wondering if it was me, or if I had any part in it, and I felt both relieved and ashamed. We kept close to our parents, all of us acting much younger and much older than we actually were. I tried to talk to Carla afterwards, but she left quickly, following her parents into the parking lot. I don't think she'd said a word to anyone.

When we returned to school, the other kids rarely talked to us, and when they did, it was about curiously un-adolescent concerns: the wet weather, the likelihood of everyone getting sick, the new parking deck at the shopping mall in Greensboro. Carla kept to herself, walking alone to classes, eating lunch at one of the single desks by the windows. Those desks were meant to be a place of punishment, but Carla ate there willingly and the teachers didn't ask her to move. Samantha King sometimes walked past to return her lunch tray, but I never saw the two speak, never saw Carla glance her way. I made small attempts at restoring our friendship, slipping notes into Carla's locker, waiting for her after class and hoping she would stop to talk, or at least say hello, maybe smile. She mostly ignored me and I finally let her slip away. We passed the last few weeks of school moving in our different spheres, away from each other, away from the other kids. In the summer, Carla's father got a job at a pharmaceutical company in Maryland and she moved away. When school started again in September, I was alone.

During our eighth grade year, Timothy was in my math class. He sat in the front row and drew pictures out of his science book using a box of colored pencils he kept hidden under his math book. Remembering his talk of Jupiter and spiders and the expanding universe, I was curious about what he was drawing. Maybe they were illustrations of the five-chambered heart of the earthworm or the icy rings of Saturn. I spent weeks just watching him draw, thinking of what we had seen, about his mother and what she had done for Nathan Price. There was a for sale sign now in the Prices' front yard—they would soon be moving, same as Carla and her parents. My father had accepted a principalship at an elementary school in Virginia, and we too would be leaving Pilot after

Christmas, though my aunt planned to stay, to keep her apartment downtown. I watched Timothy draw and thought of how, in a few months, he would be the only witness remaining, the only one who had seen Nathan Price walking across the street on his hands. The insecticides plant had just announced it was closing at the end of the year; soon, everything would be changed.

One morning, I was early to class and found Timothy alone at his desk with his colored pencils. As I moved past him to my seat, I paused to examine his paper. He'd sketched a large red sphere with pale purple lines set in a shaky grid pattern. Blurs of blue and gray were smudged across the center.

"Springtime on Mars," he told me. "It's the best time to photograph the planet. See," he pointed to the smudges, "Martian canyons."

"Yes," I said, pretending to know. I wanted Timothy to think I was smart, though I wasn't sure why. I imagined him riding the bus home in the afternoons and walking up the street to his house at the end of our street. I saw the house, pictured him inside, sketching scenes from outer space at the kitchen table while Elise cooked at the stove in her stocking feet, her shoes abandoned at the door. My aunt didn't talk about Elise Stanley after the accident; people watched her for a while, falling silent when she walked past them at the A&P, not meeting her eyes in the line at the post office. Sometimes, the other kids talked about the dead boy from Pilot, and about Davis Croswell who was the bus driver that day, even about Larry Phillips who helped push the bus away. They never said Elise Stanley's name, though, and they never talked about what she had done.

"It's nice," I told him, keeping my voice low. Some of the other kids had drifted into the room and they sat sideways at their desks, watching me, unused to hearing me speak.

I began to move towards my seat, then changed my mind. I leaned down and whispered, "Do you ever think about it? Does your mother?"

He laid his pencil on his desk and squinted up at me. It had only been a little over five months since the accident, but he seemed much older to me. His freckles had faded somewhat and his hair was more rust than red these days. Though Timothy seemed to be caught up in his own world most of the time, I knew he had friends. He had fallen into a group of boys who pierced their ears with safety pins and cut class to smoke pot behind the ball field after lunch. Timothy kept his hair shorter than the rest and he didn't wear ripped jeans, but he sat with them at lunch and rattled the chain-link fence with the others at football games. He kept himself a little apart from them, and I knew that he had that in him, a manner of separateness. I thought we were alike in that way—him, me, Elise, and even Nathan. I looked down at Timothy's Mars and hoped he would see this, that in his answer to my question, he would offer me the connection.

"It's like this," he said after a moment's pause. He tapped his pencil to one of the perfect lines on the planet's surface. "You see this?" he asked. "For years, people imagined they saw canals dug into the planet's surface. They called these canals proof of life. They worried what intelligent life on Mars might mean to us earthlings, to our safety. But, it was nothing. An optical illusion, a cosmic misprint. There's no life. There's nothing." He traced his finger over the lines. Timothy closed his notebook and began to slide his colored pencils back into their case. He glanced quickly around the room at the other kids sitting down at their desks, laughing and talking, unzipping their backpacks, taking books out. The bell rang.

"That's all there ever is," he said, "just fear."

The teacher had come in now, and I found my seat in the back of the classroom. I felt the other kids staring at me, curious. Some looked away; others kept their gazes even, slack-jawed, contemptuous. I opened my notebook and began to copy the problems from the board, my face sticky with tears I didn't try to stop.

In the years since, I have returned to Pilot only once, to attend Aunt Martha's wedding last summer. Aunt Martha, well into her fifties now, wore a pale blue dress and carried calla lilies, their stems tied together with a satin ribbon. At the reception, she joked to me that she had considered going barefoot on the grass behind the church since it was July, not a breath of wind that wasn't stifled and damp. She winked at her new husband, a mechanical engineer from Raleigh, and he raised his glass of champagne in response. I thought of my own husband, my John, back at home, and I wondered if he had given the girls their baths yet, if they were already tucked into bed and he was sitting up in his easy chair with a newspaper closed in his lap, his mind drifted to other things. We were having trouble in our marriage and he had encouraged me to take some extra time on my trip to think things through. He said I had turned into a ghost, floating along with no firm conviction that I belonged in my life. John believes in owning yourself the same way you own a car or a house, by the act of possessing.

After seeing the newlyweds off, I kissed my parents good-bye and went for a drive in our old neighborhood. The sky was just losing light and the heavy boughs of oak trees along the sides of the road appeared purple. The sidewalks were empty, and I imagined all the people curled up in the houses, different in my memory only in their diminished size—I could now fit each of them into the palm of my hand. I drove past our old house. The paint was faded and the shrubs were overgrown and straggly. Further down the street, the clearing by our old bus stop was thick with kudzu grown over tree stumps and across the grass. Here, the sun had filled up the asphalt when the bus was pushed away, the spot where Nathan Price lay, Elise Stanley hovered over him. I slowed the car, but I didn't stop, knowing this was exactly the sort of thing John had in mind that I might ponder over, a childhood tragedy I should revisit, one I had never told him about. Yet, it was here that I learned the very opposite of what John would have me believe. Nathan Price's death had only taught me that existence was made of flimsy stuff, of a cold spring morning wind, of weak sunlight. I rolled the car window down and breathed deep, the air full of failing sunlight and thick oak branches. Then, I moved on.

I came to Elise Stanley's house and parked on the opposite side of the street. My elbow propped on the open window, I took in this house that was always dark, even during the day. I knew nothing of Timothy or Elise since my family moved away, but I was certain that if Elise had left Pilot, Aunt Martha would have told me. The house was quiet and still, one light shining from inside, a circle of trees gathered around it. I could see little, only a bit of the roof, a corner of the window.

My eyes became accustomed to the dark and I made out two shapes sitting on the front steps. Likely, Timothy, in his thirties now, had moved away, at least out of his mother's house. He could have drifted off to any corner of the globe. The figures I made out might have been Elise and a man, practically a stranger to her if the rumors Aunt Martha used to tell held any truth. The shadows leaned into each other, and I could hear them talking though I couldn't distinguish the words. I thought of going to them, of finally speaking with Elise, and I went so far as to open my car door and step out. I turned to the house, and one of them stood. Elise Stanley. Her features were obscured by the shadows of the trees in the scant light, but I saw her black hair, the outline of her body, her legs. She and her companion had stopped talking, and she was looking at me, raising her arm to gesture something like hello, or come on over. At the tips of her fingers, there was a parting in the tree boughs, and a dusky, clean sky showed itself, a star there shining, just getting started in the first glimpse of night. I lifted my arm to wave back at her, remembering how she had whispered to Nathan as he lay in the street, and now I knew what she had said. I knew it because I had said the same things to my own children, whispering to them in their instances of greatest fear, them arising from a nightmare or from a simple fear of darkness, of the bleakness of things unseen. Elise had hushed that boy, holding his hurts for her own, same as any of us have done with our own children. She had completed her task—she had loved Nathan Price.

I slid back into the car, started it up, and left her there on her front steps, peering out at the street.

# The Billy Story

Stan interrupts my story and says, "Ah, the famous Billy." He rests his meaty forearms on the heavy wood table and laughs, in love with this story. We're at a steakhouse on a Saturday night with a portion of Stan's family. The Portion, an older couple from Indiana, has asked us to tell how we met, but Stan wants me to start earlier than that, years earlier, all the way back to my ex-husband, a man Stan never met.

"Or should I say, the *infamous* Billy," he says.

Two weeks after we were married, Billy rushed into our trailer in the middle of the afternoon, hours before I expected him home from work at my daddy's garage across town. He stood in the doorway and yelled out my name before he noticed me right there in front of him. I was sitting on the couch, clipping coupons from the Sunday paper.

He said, *Come on, Mindy.*

His dark eyes were twitchy, wild, and his forehead was shiny with sweat, though it was cold outside that day, much colder than usual for our town, tucked between the mountains, protected. It was chilly inside the trailer, too. Even with the kerosene heater going, I had to wear two pairs of socks and huddle under a blanket to stay warm. They were calling for snow on the radio, and at first I thought that was why Billy had come home so early.

I said, *But Billy, it's not supposed to start until later.*

*Mindy*, he hissed. *Come on.* He was still standing in the open doorway, the cold air coming in all around him. *Now*, he said, and I finally understood that there was some kind of trouble. I got up, reached for my coat, and followed Billy out the front door, leaving my scissors on the tomato box we used as a coffee table, a mess of coupons and newspapers on the floor. I didn't even switch off the lights or check to make sure I'd turned the stove off after the soup I'd heated up for my lunch. We hurried outside, the cold hitting my face and stinging my eyes. Billy helped me down the porch steps, then opened the passenger-side door of his '72 Pinto and held my hand to steady me as I clumsily lowered myself onto the seat, one hand on the top of the car, icy-cold and gritty, the other hand on my big belly. I was eight months along.

"The *infamous* Pinto," Stan says, laughing. Turning to the Portion, he adds, "She was driving an old pick-up when I met her. First thing I did for her was to buy her a decent car. Not much to look at, but it's reliable." He raps his knuckles lightly on the table and says yes to the waitress who wants to know if she should fill his water glass, and do we need a few more minutes to look over the menu? The Portion knew Stan from when he was a little boy, out on his parents' dairy farm. The man, white-haired and thick-cheeked, nods at Stan, agreeing that there are few things in life more important than a reliable automobile. The woman, dark-haired and pale-faced, smiles kindly at me and smoothes her napkin across her lap. The waitress stands there blinking at us, unsure of what to do until we open our menus to dismiss her. She is blonde and petite, young enough to have a carelessly perfect body. Pretty. She seems a little unsure of herself, giving us a hesitant smile as she leaves our table, and I wonder if this is her first day on the job.

Stan leans back in his chair and looks at me. "What a piece of shit that car must have been."

Billy headed west, pushing hard to get that old Pinto up the mountains. He coaxed it, *Come on, Baby*, and squeezed his fingers around the steering wheel. Baby crawled, her motor straining against those mountains that looped and lifted all around each other, as tangled up as a highway can be. I punched at the heater buttons but the warm air came out weak, so I hugged my coat tighter and tried not to think about how cold I was. It unsettled me to leave the trailer like that, so sudden. I asked Billy what was going on, but he wouldn't tell me. He said, *It's nothing you want to know about.*

I remembered what my daddy had told me a few weeks earlier, him knocking on my bedroom door the night before me and Billy were to get married. He said, *Mindy. This isn't right.* When I first found out I was pregnant, I couldn't look at him. I had to just look past him and never meet his eyes or else I wouldn't be able to do this, any of this. But now, I grabbed his hand and said, *Here. Feel this. The baby's moving.* I tried to put his hand on my belly, but he pulled away and said, *Listen to me. Mindy, listen.* He laid his hands on my shoulders and looked into my eyes. *That boy's been stepping out on you. There's a woman, up near Bryson.* But I knew all about Lucy Grice. She had a tattoo, the tiniest, most perfect rose you could imagine, right there on her shoulder blade. I had seen it once myself, her wearing a tank top cut in a T at the back the time I went out to the pool hall with Billy. Daddy couldn't tell me anything about Billy because I already knew. I told him, *Billy's a criminal.* He let go and stepped back, looking at me like I was something amazing and horrifying at the same moment. I said, *He robbed a gas station out in Georgia. That's how come he moved here.* I was a person falling a long ways off a bridge to my daddy. He couldn't look away. I tried to tell him about how when Billy appeared, it was like he'd come from nowhere and was the answer to a question I'd long worked to figure out. My mother had left us by then and I knew I'd rather drop out to get married than to stay home with the little ones. I thought that if I married Billy, had my own baby, I had a chance of getting out of Ezekial. Billy had big dreams for us, said we'd someday live out west where there was nothing but sunshine or else up north where everything was concrete and huge. He told me there was no limit to what we could do once he got enough money to take us—me, him, and the baby—away from this town. I couldn't say any of that to my daddy, though. Couldn't say *mom* or *leave*. I only whispered, *He's magic, Daddy.*

I glance at Stan, but he just stares down at his silverware, still wrapped up tight in a paper napkin. The Portion looks at him too, like they can't believe my confession. But Stan stays quiet, and I know he's a little hurt, hearing this about me and Billy. This is the only way I'll tell the story, though, only straight through and true to what I remember. I have to say this, about Billy and the way he talked to me and the way I believed him, to get to the part Stan is waiting for, the part where Billy leaves behind the kind of woman who needs a man to buy her a Toyota, a woman whose needs are only that—a reliable car and a man to buy it for her.

I asked Billy, *Have you done something? Have you done something wrong?*

He looked straight ahead and whispered, *That's right, Baby.*

I went back to the heater, pressing the buttons and flipping the switch back and forth from low to high, a faded red crescendo above the dial. The dial clicked, like it was trying to do something, but nothing came out of the vents.

*Shit, Billy, how long have you had this car?* I asked.

"Too damn long," Stan quips.

The waitress returns to take our order, though she approaches us with her eyebrows raised a little, tentative, ready to be turned away a second time. Her nametag says Phyllis, but she's too young for that name. She can't be more than sixteen, seventeen years old. I imagine there was a mix-up, that there's a gray-haired waitress with a name like Tiffany or Caitlin pinned to her uniform somewhere in the crowded restaurant, moving briskly and expertly from table to table, walking quickly to stop the pain of her varicose veins from throbbing in her legs. Stan, closing his menu, catches my eye and winks at me when it's my turn to order. We're all in the mood for steak tonight, each of us wanting it cooked to different extremes. The Portion, sensing the danger between me and Stan has passed, is already bored with this story, especially the man, who coughs into his fist and whose eyes peer over the top of my head, looking out across the restaurant. His wife lines up her silverware next to her plate and tilts her head, watching me. Having taken our orders, Phyllis swishes away from our table, tucking her ordering pad into her apron.

"A 1972 Pinto," Stan says with a low whistle.

Billy didn't answer me. It was getting grayer out, the clouds pressing down on us, and then it began to snow, very softly across the highway, sticking to the grass and clumps of bushes growing next to the guardrails. The sun was choked up in the clouds. There was almost no traffic on the highway, just an occasional car crawling by, more often a truck, us slipping around them, moving beyond, into the white. We swooped around the outside of the mountain and I looked out over the side, but there was only fog. If Billy had a radio that worked, it would tell us that visibility was down to almost nothing. It would say we should go home. Thinking of home sent a tingle of fear down my spine. I knew from the way Billy was acting something awful was looking for us back there.

I asked Billy, *Are you sure?*

He said, *Am I sure about what?*

*Are you sure it's nothing I want to know about?*

*That's right*, he said, nodding. He reached over to touch my face. I caught his hand and held it; his fingers were ice-cold. I couldn't believe Billy could just drive like that, naked fingers to the freezing air. I pulled them to my mouth and kissed them. He smiled and tightened his fingers around mine. He loved it when I did things like that, when I cooked him breakfast or brushed a piece of hair out of his eyes, when I washed his clothes or took his hand, anytime I did any of those things. *You're so fucking nice*, he told me once.

Billy was more relaxed then, though he kept his attention fixed on the highway, the Pinto climbing up and around. The snow was thicker, but still fluffy-like, the way a summer cloud looks from far down below on the ground. It spread out white on the highway. I wondered what Billy wanted beyond the mountains. He had told me everything was over between him and Lucy, but now I wondered if it wasn't something he'd done to her that we were running from. I met her once, when me and Billy first got engaged and he took me out to the pool hall out near the highway to celebrate. Lucy watched Billy kiss my belly first, then my hand, my elbow, my cheeks, my nose, my chin. My face hurt from smiling so much, and yet I couldn't stop, everything seemed so perfect, even with our being there, at that trashy pool hall with Lucy Grice. Billy nodded at her and said, *Have you met my girl?* He was a little drunk by then, red-faced and clumsy. Lucy leaned on her pool stick, blowing smoke up towards the ceiling. She let her eyes settle on mine for a moment before she flicked the ashes off her cigarette and turned away.

I told Billy, *I used to have a crush on this guy named Roger Coffey.* This was a lie. My crush had been on my English teacher Mr. Irving who I called Gary when no one else was around. *He asked me to marry him, you know? But it was all for fun.* I laughed. *He called me up and said, 'Mindy Grant, will you marry me?' He was just teasing me, laughing and such. Laughing because I used to like him so much.* What Gary really said was, *It's a shame, you young girls having babies. It's a damn shame.* I was too smart for this, he told me. Pretty too, he said.

*Lucky for me, you're over him*, Billy said, but I could tell he was only half-listening to me, looking out over the sweeps of curving highway in front of us, taking us somewhere only Billy knew about, the snow falling into the windshield like stars rushing to earth.

*Is it something bad?* I asked. *What you've done?*

He shook his head and sighed, like it was no big deal and I should just let it go, and I thought again about asking him about Lucy. She was older than me and Billy, nearly thirty though the heavy make-up she wore made her look closer to forty. Her looks were the opposite of mine. She was tall to my shortness, dark to my paleness, angular and bony where I was soft and flabby, more and more so as the baby grew inside me. *You're pregnant everywhere*, one of the Baptist ladies observed, then winked at me as if she'd told me a secret. Daddy said, *He's making a fool out of you, girl*.

The food arrives, Phyllis hurrying to set the plates in front of us, still tentative in her movements, unsure of who ordered what. Stan teases me, "Is that slab of meat big enough for you?" He knows it's too much. I slice open my baked potato and watch the steam escape. The Portion politely begins cutting their steaks up into tiny pieces while Stan chews and nods enthusiastically at how good the food is. He grins at me and I lift my knife, cut into my steak which is too pink. "Everything all right?" he asks me. I nod and take a bite, not wanting to cause Phyllis any trouble. Stan laughs, "The infamous Billy, my predecessor." He points a fork-full of meat across the table at the Portion, shaking his head, amused. He drinks his tea, sets the glass down on the gleaming wood table.

"Let's hear the rest," he says.

The snow kept snowing. After a while, it became a single thing, each piece coming close behind the one before. Watching it fall made me colder. I couldn't believe there was a warm place anywhere, that our trailer still existed. I thought about the coupons scattered on the carpet, the scissors laid on the makeshift coffee table. I couldn't remember if the radio was on or not. I imagined it was. I pictured the kerosene heater, heating nothing but empty space.

*Billy.* I sat up in my seat. *Billy. We left the heater on.*
*What?*
*The kerosene heater. We have to go back.*
Billy gripped the steering wheel. *Come on, Baby,* he whispered. I could tell he was angry, that he was trying to tune me out. He narrowed his eyes on the highway and I knew what he was doing. He wanted the highway to be the only thing. He'd once told me that it was the purest way to live—on a highway, not here, not there, only and always in between. He had been through twelve states before he ended up in Ezekial, working in my daddy's garage. Daddy said he couldn't fix a car for nothing, that he couldn't even change a spark plug. He kept Billy on for my benefit. *How else,* Daddy said, *is that son of a bitch going to feed my daughter?*
*Billy.*
*That's right, Baby. You're doing just fine. That's right.* His voice was tight and thin.
*Shit, Billy. Did you hear me? I left the heater on. Billy, we have to go back.*
*No.*
*The whole trailer's going to burn to the ground.*
*It doesn't matter.*
*What the hell, Billy?*
*Oh, yeah?* he asked, turning excitedly to me. *Oh, yeah?* The car swerved as he looked back and forth between me and the road. *You want to know, do you?* He jerked the steering wheel to the left and slammed on the brakes. The car fishtailed and veered across the highway. Everything spun. We turned around and around in the blank space, the ground white, the sky white. We're falling through the air, I thought, but we weren't. I could feel the tires beneath us, spinning, searching for something to grip onto.

"Magic you say," Stan snorts. He cuts another piece of steak, chews vigorously. "Magic." He's not going to let it go after all.

Finally, the car slammed against the guard rail. I put both hands on my belly.

*This*, Billy said, reaching into the back seat and pulling out a paper grocery bag. *Here it is.* I can't open my eyes to see what he's showing me. I thought about the coupons in the trailer, burned to nothing. I thought about the couch, the tomato box, the blanket I used to cover up with, all gone. Every bit of it nothing but cinders, something for the firemen to sift through, looking for the cause. Billy opened the bag over my head and I felt bits of something coming down on my shoulders. Could it be—ashes? I saw the trailer burning, the windows melting, the carpet ablaze. I opened my eyes and looked. Money. I collected the bills in my hands, smoothing them down with my numb fingers. Twenties, tens, ones.

*There*, he said. There. *Your daddy don't keep much in the register.*

I shook my head. *Hush.*

"Magic money," Stan scoffs, eating the last of his steak. The Portion has left part of their dinners on their plates. I catch the woman looking quickly at me, wondering about this wife of Stan's with such a past. Of course, we all know why I've told all this, why Stan wanted me to, him figuring it into the story of us. The moral of the story, the thing I should always remember, is how thankful I am that Stan found me. I was saved, that is the lesson.

I kept my hands on my belly. *Hush*, I said. *I can't feel the baby move.* I was still and quiet, waiting. I wouldn't even look at Billy. I finally felt a tiny thump, like a hiccup. I said, *The whole trailer's burned down.*

*It doesn't matter*, he said again, and tried to crank the engine.

*No*, I said. *Take me home.*

"Famous last words," Stan says, winking at me.

Phyllis comes and clears our table. I've hardly touched my food. She wants to know if we're interested in dessert tonight but we just want coffee. Her eyes catch mine for just a second and I smile at her, wanting some spark of connection, some way of telling her that I understand something about who she is, young and working here, so much else she could be doing. I watch her swish away from our table and I wonder where she'll go when she gets off work, if she still lives at home or if she's on her own yet. I look around the restaurant to see if there are any teenaged boys looking for her, maybe just one waiting for her to finish her shift, but there's nobody young here, just Phyllis.

"That's how it all ended," Stan says.

Of course, that wasn't the end, not the way Stan means. But I stop talking here and play the rest of the events in my head, remembering Billy swearing and beating the steering wheel with his fists when the car wouldn't crank. He was real anxious about it, looking out the window at all that snow, and I knew the car was stolen, that someone in Georgia or Maine was missing a 1972 Pinto, that there was no telling what all Billy had taken, where all he had been. He tried again and again but all Baby would do was sputter and die each time. Finally, he told me, *Stay put*. He gathered up the money, put some in his pocket and the rest in my freezing fingers, then kissed my forehead before he slammed the door closed and walked away. He didn't even lie to me, didn't say he would come back for me. I watched him disappear into the white.

As we sip our coffee, Stan rubs my knee under the table. He says, "Whatever it took to get you to me." The Portion smiles at us. I squeeze Stan's hand, but then pull away. I want to be alone, inside my own mind for the end of the story.

Stan says, "We met five years later. She was working at a supermarket."

It grew even colder as I waited in the car, the sky becoming darker and darker. I had fallen asleep by the time someone finally came, but it wasn't Billy. It was a police officer with a brown mustache and a big, crooked nose. He said he couldn't believe I was out there all by myself. He asked me if there was anyone else and I told him no. *I was trying to get to the hospital*, I explained. I pointed to my belly and let him think I was in labor. The officer nodded, said nothing of my being in the passenger seat and nothing more of the missing driver.

## Springtime on Mars

On the way to the hospital, Officer Pugh—that was his name—turned his blue-lights on and told me to rest easy. The lights flashed against the white snow and blued up the trees. To get my mind off everything, he told me about his family. He had a little girl, barely four years old. *She's a mess*, he said and laughed good-naturedly. *But, she's my heart, you know what I mean?* I told him I did. We turned off the highway and I looked out the window, watching the snow fall under the street lights, searching the black spaces in between, and feeling Billy, gone now.

# Radio Vision

The boys went back to school the Tuesday after President Kennedy was shot, and Marianne Binger set about her chores that morning in numb automation. There was a comforting efficiency to wiping down the gold-specked Formica countertop and setting just-rinsed breakfast dishes in the drainer to dry. The house was full of its smells: the earthy remnant of dirty boy smell, the hot smell of the television set lighting its phosphor-coated tubes in the living room, her own heavy-scented cigarettes, smoked down to the filter, and the stridently pine scent of Airwick, set out to mask the cigarettes. Marianne was absolutely addicted to Airwick. The president had been shot in broad daylight, and she listened now for the sound of Russian aircraft to descend. It might have been Castro.

The boys were nine years old, twins. They were active little boys, though Peter was more rambunctious than his brother. Luke was introspective and calm like their father, the Reverend Joe Binger. At times, Marianne was yet surprised to find herself married to a preacher.

She settled into a cup of coffee and a cigarette at the kitchen table, looking out the window at the autumn maple, its leaves lit gold by the sun. Everything seemed changed. Wrapping her fingers around the warm mug, Marianne thought about Jackie Kennedy, that stately woman in her blood-spattered designer suit. She thought of her beautiful face, smooth and pale, and how her beauty made her sadness all the more painful. Yes, the country was in mourning, but it was Jackie Kennedy who had suffered such a personal loss, the loss of her handsome, youthful husband, gone before her eyes.Marianne shuddered. What if some terrible tragedy should take her Joe away? Would her sadness be as poignant, as achingly beautiful as this woman's grief?

Joe spent most of his evenings at his workbench in the basement, baffling over the innards of the transistor radio and the telephone. He was captivated by the miracle of electricity—the idea that artificial illumination even existed yet amazed him—this man of God, awed by wonders of both supernatural workings and the mortal hand of mankind. One night last week, at dinner, he had ruminated over the inner mechanics of the atom and their parallel workings in the universe, the spinning of planets and electrons. It was all related, of course, to how the internal combustion engine worked—all of it trapped energy—that powered not only automobiles and tractors, but also roller-coasters and rocket ships. He added the last part as a means of drawing the boys into the conversation, but Luke's thoughts were clearly elsewhere, and Peter had already made a fork-tine road in his mashed potatoes and left, himself a charged bit of matter bouncing off the confines of his environment. After a moment, Luke asked to be excused and Marianne was left with her husband who stared vacantly at his water glass. She waited to see if he would say anything else, then rose to clear the dishes while Joe escaped to the basement. There, he had explained to her, he was conducting an experiment using paper clips and a live wire, pulled from the cinderblock wall.

As she snubbed out her cigarette and rinsed her cup in the sink, Marianne thought, thirty-four. One of the television commentaries had mentioned Jackie Kennedy's age and it was Marianne's age exactly. She was in this way aligned with the grieving first lady: they had seen the very same days.

She moved into the boys' room to gather dirty laundry, pausing to straighten their twin beds, to touch the river rock Luke kept on his nightstand, to pick up Peter's scouts canteen off the floor. It was a clean blue autumn day, and Marianne paused at the top of the basement stairs, the laundry basket on her hip. On Sunday, Joe had preached to the grief-shocked congregation on patriotism and closing ranks, human fear and God's protection. He closed with "The Battle Hymn of the Republic," and reassured the assembled Methodists that God was still greater than he that was against us. Marianne and the family went home, switched on the television, and watched the replays of Lee Harvey Oswald's assassination. It had happened on live television while they were at church and it seemed to Marianne the world had changed once again. The image of Jack Ruby taking two quick steps then lifting the gun had stayed with Marianne, as had the church's closing song, and that terrible ache on Jackie Kennedy's pretty face. As she descended the basement stairs, her feet bare on the cool slat steps, feeling for the switch at the bottom of the stairs, Marianne saw Jack Ruby in his tidy suit; she heard the congregation singing the hymn. The basement, dark except for the small square of light from the high window, was still and quiet and musty-smelling, the floor still damp from Saturday's rain. She wished she'd put her shoes on before coming down. *His truth was marching on.* Here was Jack Ruby's fedora, the Dallas police in a jumble, the exquisite countenance of the first lady, ashen with grief. Marianne wanted another cigarette.

At the bottom of the stairs, she stepped into a cold rain puddle to her ankles and cursed Joe—problems with the house were full on his shoulders—before her fingers found the light switch on the wall. The light flashed, then sprang on, the radio coming to life with it. Joe *had* managed that, rewiring the outlet so that it came to power with the light switch, the electricity juicing up the two separate lines at once, now escaping through a frayed wire in the puddle. Instantly, a terrific buzz snapped along Marianne's spine, her limbs, her fingertips. A blue band of cool light pressed against her eyes as she fell, the basket thudding onto the concrete floor beside her.

The second grade teacher had said his cursive S's looked like lazy swans, and Peter was still sore about it that afternoon as he walked home from school. Miss Mackey had spent much of the day tearful over the president's death, eliciting examples of patriotism from Peter's classmates, but when the children grew restless, she passed out pulpy blue-lined paper and said they would practice their penmanship. Peter wished now, as he followed the sidewalk to the street his family lived on, that he had raised his hand and said he would join the army. His twin brother Luke walked in front of him, the line of his trimmed brown hair neat against the skinny pale of his neck, glaringly white in the sun.

Too much drooping, Miss Mackey had said, correcting Peter's letters with her own tall, looping S's. Luke had once said Miss Mackey was pretty, but Peter didn't believe this was true. Luke had only said it because he could write perfect swans, necks tall and slender, neatly rounded bellies gliding along. Peter shuffled a few paces behind his brother and pictured himself and his mother at the kitchen table tonight after dinner, him practicing the letters until he got them just right, his mother sitting close to him and nodding, yes, that's good. During the weekend, she had been small and quiet, sobbing soundlessly over the president's funeral, but this morning, she had seemed better and Peter thought of her smoking her thin, white cigarettes and smiling at him over his letters. Very good, she would say. Maybe he would tell her of his plans to join the army.

"Miss Mackey looks like a duck," Peter said.

"No," Luke answered without turning around to look back at him, "Miss Mackey doesn't waddle. She doesn't *quack*."

Springtime on Mars

Their mother wasn't in the kitchen when they arrived home, and Luke switched off the television to listen for her. The boys felt the house's emptiness at once and looked at each other, wondering where she might be. Though it was not unusual for her to lose track of time while having coffee at a neighbor's or to get caught up running errands downtown, Peter felt uneasy. He feared something awful had happened to her, but he knew better than to mention it to his brother who would only tease him and call him a baby. Though they were identical twins, dressed alike and with matching haircuts, most of the people in their neighborhood and at their church, at least their classmates and the handful or so of adults who knew them well, could distinguish them by the way they held their faces, their shoulders, by the volume of their voices. Luke spoke in low, measured tones while Peter was excitable, red-faced and perspiring. The world seemed to favor Luke, especially their father and Miss Mackey and an entire array of Sunday School teachers.

It usually fell on Luke to make the decisions, and Peter looked at him now, wondering what they would do with this unexpected freedom. The afternoon was still; the furnace clicked off and the house was full of quiet. Peter wanted to go outside and play Cowboys and Indians. They had not been allowed to play outside all weekend for the rain and the somberness of the president's death, and now he wanted very badly to escape. He would have to be the cowboy, who always got scalped in the end, or else Luke would refuse to play. The scalping was done with their mother's old spatula, taken from the kitchen and stored in a tin barrel along with a dozen pine cone hand grenades, a few homemade sling shots, an arsenal of rocks, and an old hymnal Luke had swiped from the choir dressing room for no good reason that Peter could imagine. Sometimes, Luke was as much a mystery to Peter as their father was.

Peter suggested Cowboys and Indians, even volunteering outright to be the cowboy, but Luke shook his head. He squinted at

133

his brother, his thumbs hooked into his belt loops, and said, "We'll have a séance for Jimmy Bowen."

Jimmy Bowen was a boy who had disappeared years ago, when their mother was a girl. He went missing from Carson, Tennessee, hometown to both of their parents. Now they lived in Michigan. Their mother loved to tell the boys stories of her girlhood in the mountains and the tale of Jimmy Bowen was one of her favorites. On summer days, young people crowded around Brown Lake, which was actually just a smallish pool of water caught between two mountains. The boys swam while the girls sunned themselves on the cool rocks and muddy beaches. Their mother, only thirteen at the time, was propped up on her elbows and watching the water. One minute, there was Jimmy Bowen, splashing around with the other teenaged boys, throwing a football hard enough to make the other boys flinch, and then, he was gone. If he drowned, no one saw him slip beneath the water, no one saw him struggle. If he waded back out of the water and wandered away, no one saw him leave. One of the other boys started to throw the football to him, another called out, *Bowen!,* and then they saw that he wasn't there. He simply—their mother snapped her fingers—vanished.

Peter didn't want to have the séance. He had never seen his mother cry so much as she had the past few days. On Saturday, it had rained heavily all day and his mother had stared out the window and said they would need a boat to get out in weather like this. Even their father seemed shaken, his long thin fingers trembling a little as he searched his Bible for the scripture reading during Sunday service.

Peter said, "Mom won't let us."

Luke blinked back at him and wordlessly went for his river rock, the one he'd taken from Tennessee last summer when they'd gone to visit their grandparents and their mother had told them the story. He took a set of candles from the kitchen drawer and the crystal candlesticks from the china cabinet. They had always held their Jimmy Bowen séances in the hall bathroom because it was the smallest room in the house and because it was the only room where either of them was allowed any privacy. Even if it was the middle of the night, as it usually was when they lit the candles and sat on the cool tile, the river rock on the floor between them, their mother, if she woke, would knock on the other side of the door, and then pause before she pushed the door open. This alone made it the ideal place, though Luke said spirits from beyond the grave didn't like mirrors.

"It won't work in the daytime," Peter said, but Luke pulled the curtains over the narrow window above the toilet and said they would try it anyway. "Ghosts," Peter said, "don't like to be seen." Luke said the ghosts *did* like to be seen, that that was the point of holding a séance in the first place. It was dark enough, Luke decided, with the curtains pulled and the door closed.

They began. Luke rolled up the bathroom rug and set the stone on the floor with the candles on either side. He struck a match to light the candles then sat with his hands lifted, insisting Peter touch the tips of his fingers to his. They closed their eyes and sat silently for a long moment. Luke believed Jimmy would enter the bathroom without an actual spoken invitation. Peter had pointed out that they didn't know for sure that Jimmy was dead, but Luke just shook his head impatiently. Of course the boy was dead. This had happened years ago.

"Sit still," Luke instructed. "Listen."

Peter had forgotten his misshapen swans from earlier in the day and concerned himself now with what the ghost of a boy from Tennessee, so long dead, would have to say. He thought the boy might not want to be called away from heaven. The flicker of the candles bothered Peter and he kept his eyes half-open, alert to the shadows in the room. He could hear the trees shake their dry leaves in the breeze outside the window. If the boy wasn't in heaven, he was a demon from below and he would want to hurt them. Peter thought his fiery fingers could reach through his scalp, his skull, and melt his brain away.

Their father had said it was a sin to try to contact the dead. There had been a rash of Ouija boards among the neighborhood youth the year before and he had preached against such practices, claiming it was all party to the occult. From the pulpit he asked, Child's play or Satan's handiwork? Their mother said, "Jimmy Bowen was the first boy I ever took a liking to."

If Jimmy Bowen did appear, Peter imagined he would come to them in something called radio vision, the link between radio and television. His father had told him about how this had been used long ago to broadcast the hazy image of President Hoover to an audience in New York City who couldn't understand what was happening to them. To them, it seemed like a haunting, like Armageddon, their president coming to speak to them, nothing like technology. Peter didn't know how his father knew such things.

He stole a glance at his brother, wanting to ask him if their father had ever told him about the first television. But Luke bore a look of concentration, his eyes clamped shut, his mouth slightly open, his fingertips trembling against Peter's. Once, he claimed the rock had twitched there on the floor though Peter had not seen it happen. Also, he had once heard the dead boy's voice, yet Peter had heard nothing, only the rain against the windows, the refrigerator humming, Bucky, the neighbor's dog, barking. Luke had believed Jimmy Bowen was speaking to them, that he longed to tell them something.

"It won't work," Peter whispered now, but Luke only furrowed his brow in answer, as if straining to hear the ghost.

With the sound of his own voice, the spell had been broken and Peter was no longer afraid. He took his fingers away from his brother's and began passing them over one of the candles, pinching his fingers closed just above the flame. He was bored and began to think again about playing Cowboys and Indians. He thought he could insist on being the Indian now—no, the Indian *chief*—since he had endured the séance, and he became restless, thinking of the fine, clear day outside, his legs aching to stand up, to run. He passed his fingers over the flame once again, this time bringing his fingertips too low and searing the pads of his thumb and his forefinger. He cried out in pain, yanking his burned fingers to his mouth.

Luke's eyes snapped open. "Did you see him?"

"It's evil," Peter said, recalling their father's words. He sucked on his burned fingers and cried.

Luke blew out the candles and pulled himself up, standing now before the mirror. He stood looking there for a long moment and when nothing happened, he told Peter to stop crying. He knelt to hold the rock in his hands for a moment, then solemnly looked up at his brother and said, "It's warm. There's energy trapped here." They gathered the candles and the crystal candlesticks and replaced the rug on the bathroom floor. Everything was put back in order and the boys looked around the house. Their mother had not yet returned home.

"Maybe she's gone to the market," Peter said. "Or, maybe, she's having coffee with Mrs. Bailey."

Luke moved to the hallway; the basement door was open. The boys hadn't noticed it before and now they stood back, staring at it. Peter remembered that something bad might have happened to his mother. One of his classmates had whispered to him today in the lunchroom that the Communists would not stop at just killing the president. Their mother disliked being in the basement and only went there to do the wash. She insisted on keeping the door shut to keep the mice out of the house and she was always reminding their father, who went to his worktable in the basement most evenings after dinner, to close it.

"The wash," Peter said, but Luke gestured for him to keep quiet. He stood peering down the stairs for a moment before he put his hand on the rail and stepped down, into the stairwell. He kept one hand behind him as he moved slowly down the steps, as if to hold his brother back. Peter whispered, "Is she down there?" but Luke shook his head: he was listening for something. The basement was dark. Truthfully, Peter didn't like going down there any more than their mother did, though he sometimes went there to join their father, to look over the tangle of wires and telephone pieces, bits of plastic and metal. His father was only a Methodist preacher, but some day he would invent something like a robot that could drive cars or a television in a booth, images and sounds flashing all around. All of that was before the president had been shot and their mother had said everything was different now; the whole world was changed. Peter considered going back now, but he did not want to be alone, not even in the living room with its pinkish-gray late afternoon light coming through the windows. He wished Luke would say something, and Peter tried once again, "She went to the bank. She just forgot." But Luke had seen something now and stopped on the steps.

There was just the one window in the basement, weak sunlight coming through, and the boys had to allow their eyes a moment to adjust before they could see her. She lay at the bottom, her skirt around her, her face almost completely covered by her hair. Peter wanted to go to her, but Luke held him back. He sensed some sort of danger, some lingering bad spirit called from the dead. Later, he would say it was Jimmy Bowen, come to take their mother even before the wordless invitation of the séance. Spirits from the other side, he would later explain, don't like to be bothered by the living. He would take the spirit-warmed rock into the woods and leave it there, as an anchor to Jimmy Bowen's wandering spirit. The boys' father would rarely speak of his wife's death, and their neighbors would wonder at what had befallen them, first the president killed in Dallas and now, Marianne Binger in her own basement? There was no safe place after all.

But Peter knew from the first that he was the reason for this. It was the fact of his messy existence, the undeniable line of crumpled swans. His own insistent surge into the universe had crowded his mother out of being. He thought of the little boy in the powder blue jacket who saluted the fallen leader, how his mother had cried at the sight. There was no president, only Peter's mother, her face pressed against the gritty basement floor.

# Zenith, 1954

We stood on the bright lawn and watched the delivery boys struggle up the outside stairs with the cumbersome wooden box fitted with shiny knobs and a twenty-five inch screen. It was a brand-new Zenith, the best money can buy.

Laney nudged me, whispered, "What'll we do with it?"

Joe kept back, arms folded, unsure of whether he should help the delivery boys, two local teenagers. My husband was a tall, solid-looking man who often worried over being useless. It was our first year pastoring in Oliver, and the church elders had made a gift of the television set to me and the Reverend Joe. Though I knew he did not want to accept it, he could not refuse. It was a tranquil Saturday morning. He rocked on his heels and squinted into the sky, so blue it was almost indecent to look at.

"I expect it'll be good for us, Miss Laney," I told her. Laney, a widow, was our landlady. She lived in the apartment below ours. Her cottony white hair was coming out of its bun in wisps and sticking to her pale temples, glistening pink now in the heat. I was in my seventh month of pregnancy, twins. The morning sickness had not left me in the first months as it did other women, and the stench of the turkey farms outside town simmered in the summer temperatures. I held my belly to steady myself, still grinning at Laney, teasing her a little. "I expect we'll finally have something to amuse ourselves with," I told her.

Joe frowned. "Marianne," he said, lifting his eyebrows, but that was all. The delivery boys labored to fit the television set through our apartment door and Joe rushed to help. When I was a girl, I saw a boy disappear into a river. I was lying on the bank with my sisters, the oldest chattering about her upcoming wedding and me feeling far away from such things, just watching that boy sparkling like a coin out there in the water, gold and slick. He slipped away and then, there was Joe, standing in front of the church some years later, a man of God taking his hand at preaching. I had to marry Joe while he was still that way, so certain of things to come. Now, watching him stand above us while the delivery boys eased the chunk of metal and mahogany into our tiny living room, I felt something stopped up inside of me, some fear even Joe's unshakeable faith couldn't temper. The houses lining the street behind us were smudged and loose in the beaming sun.

"They have the stories," I said, taking Laney's thin elbow and stepping towards the house. Joe had followed the boys through the doorway. "In the afternoon, you and I can watch the stories together," I said. Laney nodded. As we went, she leaned into me, slightly winded, her breath smelling of black licorice and coffee, her bones small and hollow-feeling—like a bird's—next to my own heavy body, thick with hot juices, life pumping through.

Laney's trepidations were short-lived, however, and before long, watching the television was our prime activity. We started right up with *The Guiding Light.* "These stories," she said, "are overly dramatic. They carry on too much." And yet, she watched. We made sun tea sweetened with too much sugar and drank gallons of it, deliberating over the travails of the characters on the soap operas. "I once knew a girl like that," Laney said. "She left home only to return many years later." These were Laney's stories, told in the afterglow of the television, or between programs, sometimes right in the middle of them, her and me sitting together on the sofa, my pulse throbbing dully behind my eyes. She sometimes confused the details with what she'd seen on television, telling me her uncle had built a living room suite out of a block of wood. It was the same feat accomplished by a contestant on a game show, a man from Ohio sawing and hammering in his suit and tie while the audience cheered and applauded. "Her father had died," Laney continued, "and she was eat up with regret. Just like this one here." She leaned forward to stare at the screen.

Those first weeks of television, we dozed whole afternoons away. My dreams were a fog of dark, formless babies, me waking up damp with sweat, thirsty and weak. I was terrified of the babies, of what they might want from me when they came, of what might become of me if they delayed. I told Laney, "These babies won't let me be," and to Joe, I said, "I've changed my mind about all this."

The Reverend Joe ignored the television as best he could, taking to his Bible study and his newspapers at the kitchen table after dinner, emerging late to watch the stations sign off and the screen take on its testing pattern. He seemed nervous around it, glancing at the squiggly faces of the panel on *I've Got a Secret* like it was a wearisome houseguest he'd rather avoid. He said little about it, only that he hoped Laney and I weren't watching too much.

One evening, though, he came in from the kitchen and, finding Laney sleeping on the couch, he did not retreat to the hallway. He stood watching. As a boy, he'd had a scientific mind, reading all sorts of curiosities about outer space and the workings of his electric toy train. He had long since taken up with God when I first met him, but he remained mystified by the scientific world and its discoveries. I remembered cool autumn evenings when he took me up on the Parkway in his father's Buick and explained the chemistry of leaves' color change as well as the science behind the impending nuclear age. He sometimes stopped the car at an overlook and took my hand. I felt safe there, despite what he was saying about fall-out and radioactivity and the coming of uncontrolled invention.

Joe finally switched the set off. The screen wizened to a small dot of light and he stood back, watching it. "It's made by an ordered scramble of radar signals," he whispered, and I knew he'd been reading about the mechanics of the television back there at the kitchen table, among his theology guides and his newspapers. "Starting in 1927, television's first appearance." He gave a low, reverential whistle. "This baby has been in the works for quite some time."

It was dark then with the gleam of the television set gone and all I could see of my husband was his shadowy outline. The house was quiet except for Laney's soft snoring, and Joe whispered, "We need to help her downstairs."

"I've changed my mind about all this," I said for the second time, and Joe's dark person crossed the room to me. He took my hand and guided me to standing, saying he could see about getting rid of the television. I shook my head: no, we couldn't; no, that wasn't what I meant. Together we woke Laney and half-carried her downstairs. Her slippered feet padded the outside steps, the night close and rich. Joe stood outside her bedroom door while I helped her into bed. She spoke one word: Leland—her late husband's name—before closing her eyes and settling into sleep again. Joe smiled at me when I returned to him.

I was not the pastor's wife the First Methodist ladies had envisioned, these women in their plain dresses and thick-healed pumps, their lips painted Mamie Eisenhower pink. They whispered together over their cream-and-sugar coffee at Wednesday morning prayer groups, but I had little to add about how the young girls carried on at the school dances or about the snake-handling Baptists in the green hills of Picard. I could not guess what was Christian and what wasn't.

Nor would I say much about my pregnancy, godly procreation being the chief topic of conversation among the church ladies, farmer's wives, most of them; the rest worked the looms at the textile mill. Their faces were pale and doughy, their hands red and cracked from their work, but their eyes brightened at talk of babies and mingled into such discussions was the unspoken breathlessness of certain biological facts—the business of making babies was a lusty business indeed. My swollen middle was undeniable evidence of the Reverend Joe's virility. Twins, the ladies simpered, their palms flat on my belly while their eyes searched my face for clues of the preacher's secret doings, half in love with Joe themselves. He stood at the altar in the dappled light of the church windows, so unsure of himself, so sure of God, entreating his congregants to answer the highest calling of service and sacrifice. The women blinked in loving reverence and took small, unkind glances at their husbands, bored and drooping in the pews next to them. I kept the details of my back pains and heartburn to myself, tucking away the private joy of tiny thumps, the pinpricks of fear, my own heartbeats caught in my throat.

Dottie Bligh was one of the church ladies to fall in love with the Reverend Joe. She was an elder's wife, important in the church. Though Dottie was barely in her forties, there was no end to her old lady ailments, her dizzy spells and arthritis, her weak heart and chronic bronchitis. She was nearly always short of breath and weak, grasping onto pews and passersby to steady herself.

After church, she was usually the last to totter up the aisle and shake Joe's hand, leaning into him and speaking in a breathy, almost husky way she was brazen enough to do only when the church's front steps were emptied of the other congregants. Even her husband, cheerless Martin Bligh, left church before her, going out to wait in the car with the windows rolled down. I saw him out there on the Sundays Laney came to church, me helping her to the car after services. Other days, I stayed behind, going through the pews and picking up misplaced prayer cards and hymnals, tidying up in a deliberate, unhurried way. Joe looked over Dottie's shoulder, searching for me, but I kept back, pretending not to see. Later, when he questioned me, I told him I was only being careful not to interrupt the counsel of the pastor and his congregant. I said I was not interested in hearing her confessions.

But Dottie was loose with her affections and though it was clear she preferred the arm of the Reverend Joe, she often hung to my shoulder when my husband couldn't be reached. I was tending to the dessert table at a fifth Sunday potluck dinner one evening several weeks after the television had arrived. She approached me, grinning wildly—Dottie always gave the impression she was half-drunk.

"Goodness, Marianne," she said, looking down to consider my unwieldy girth, "you're coming right along, aren't you?" She wrinkled her nose to show there was something vaguely distasteful to this, my full-bloomed pregnancy. I nodded, slicing a three-layer chocolate cake into generous wedges, taking care not to severe the maraschino cherries lining the cake's perimeter. It was late in the evening since dinner had been delayed by an elders' meeting and a prolonged youth baseball game. The chocolate frosting gummed onto my knife as I worked. "It's a wonder," she said.

I murmured agreement—*life* was a wonder—and scanned the fellowship hall tables, sagging with food and coarse tablecloths and the elbows of church members. I finally spotted Joe, stopping to shake hands with Frank Schaeffer, a beefy, vigorous man who owned several real estate holdings in town and who, when it came to a vote, always favored conservative approaches to fiscal matters. I knew Frank did not hold to the elders' decision to gift us with a television set, a worthless diversion that not only inspired rampant idleness, but also one that was relatively new—the whole thing could turn out to be nothing more than a Hollywood fad. There was Joe, shaking this man's hand and trying his best to smooth the matter over, a miserable attempt to judge from Frank's short, gruff nods and bleak hesitations.

"I only gained seventeen pounds with my Murray," Dottie continued, fingering the ruffled collar of her dress. "I suppose the Reverend doesn't mind the extra pounds. Him so full of devotion, so empty of vanity and pride." She sighed and I thought of her own dull Martin whom I saw sitting near the back of the room, hunched over his plate, nodding noncommittally at something Eddie Long was saying. A few tables over, Joe released Frank's hand and began to move on to the next congregant; then, stopping, he turned back to Frank.

"The doctor says my weight is fine," I told Dottie. I had finished cutting the cake and paused to lick the excess frosting off my fingers, keeping my eye on Joe over her shoulder. "Just fine," I said. He was standing over Frank now, his hand clasped on the back of his chair, his other hand making little jabs in the air as he spoke. Joe looked agitated, his face flushed, his body tense, and some of the people in the chairs around them had stopped eating and were watching my husband. Frank gazed at his half-eaten plate of fried chicken and slowly shook his head.

"Dr. Bentley?" Dottie asked, sneering a little though I couldn't guess what insufficiency she had judged in the town's only obstetrician. "Well," she sniffed, appearing to change her mind about something, "That's fine. I'm sure, with twins..."

"Yes," I wiped my fingers on a napkin and took her hands firmly between my own. "*I'm* sure. I really must go see to the coffee." Frank had turned in his chair and was answering Joe now, his expression severe. More congregants had stopped eating to stare. I squeezed Dottie's hands, wishing her a good night, but when I tried to pull away, she held on.

"Let's have dinner," she said, her voice low, her breath moist. "We'd love to see the Zenith. I can bring a lemon bundt." Her hands were soft with rose-scented lotion, sleekly oiled flesh over the knobby bones of her fingers. Joe put his hand on Frank's shoulder. A twinge of nausea moved through me, gastric fluids rising up the back of my throat. Dottie Bligh held on. "We can come Saturday."

She released me and I moved away, hurrying through the maze of folding chairs, smiling, excuse me, excuse me, and finally getting through to Joe. Frank stood facing him. Joe was saying, "…my position here as pastor. We need to move forward, be bold in all…" and there he broke off, turning to me when I touched his arm. Frank put up his hands to show the conversation was over. "Joe," I said, pulling lightly on his arm, but he would not give up his stance. Frank sat, and Joe stood over him, his fists on his hips. "*Joe,*" I said.

After a moment, he turned and began to pick his way out of the room, chair legs scuffing against the floor as people hurried to make room for him to go by. I followed, squeezing my huge belly through the tangle of chairs and tables, all the faces looking first at Joe, then me. He went out the side door, but I hurried to the wash room where I held my wrists under cold water and waited for the sickness to subside. My face was yellow and ill-looking in the mirror. When I returned to the fellowship hall, Joe had not returned, and I stepped out into the purple-skyed dusk. He wasn't there either, and I set out, slowly, for home.

I found Laney upstairs, alone, watching a cooking show. She was in her quilted housedress and her hair was undone, coming down over her shoulders. When the program was over, I helped her to bed and sat up for Joe, remembering that horizon on the Parkway he'd shown me years ago. *None of these colors,* he'd said, pointing at the autumn trees, *are true.* I settled into bed and turned the pages of a magazine. There was an article on growing beets, another on how to discipline an unruly child. A fashion piece on the new look from London. I waited.

It was past ten, though, when I finally heard the key in the door. He walked into the bedroom and began undressing for bed without a word. I closed my magazine and watched him, his movements slow, him slipping out of his shirt, the warm, dry smell of starch still on its sleeves. He took his belt off in a long, slow glide and sat on the bed, bare-chested, wearing only his pants and his socks, looking across the room at the blue flowered wallpaper.

I found his silence unsettling. "Joe," I said, but he shook his head. I wanted to know about what had happened with Frank Schaeffer, to ask if he'd been talking to the other elders, if there were things to settle, to smooth over. I began to talk, telling him about how Dottie Bligh had cornered me. "She wants to come to dinner Saturday night. I don't think I can take all that on, a big dinner and all," I told Joe. I had managed to avoid entertaining in the months we'd lived in Oliver, and I had come to expect, especially with my due date coming so near, I could avoid it altogether, at least for a time. "There's too much to it," I explained, smoothing my nightgown over my belly. "Making a big dinner is too much work."

"Marianne," he began slowly, turning to look at me. "What makes you think I can do anything to stop her? What makes you think I can do a single thing?" His eyes shone in the soft glare of my reading lamp. He turned away, pulling his socks off and dropping them onto the floor.

"Joe," I said. "Tell me what happened."

But he would say no more, slipping his pants off and laying them on the armchair in the corner of the room. He crawled into bed and turned his back away from me. After a long moment, I switched off the light.

The next morning, Joe said the Blighs would most certainly be coming to dinner on Saturday night. "We need them," he said but then gave no further explanation. He moved across the room and laid one hand on my belly, closing his eyes for a moment like he meant to pray over our tiny babies. Then he left, the sky still dark, Laney not even up yet.

Once I relented to the inevitability of Saturday night dinner, I wore myself out with cleaning, dusting the furniture and scrubbing at the kitchen floor on my hands and knees until I was too sore and sick to do anything but stumble into bed by early afternoon. I lay in the bedroom, Laney at work in her kitchen downstairs, testing her biscuits, her having decided to present a basket of cat-heads for Saturday's dinner. Joe came in early from his church office throughout the week and shunned his newspaper and Bible study for hours of television-watching. I crept through and found him taking in, with some curiosity, the same soap operas Laney and I now missed more often than not. Other times, he watched a preacher out of Atlanta, my husband leaning forward, his elbows propped on his knees, studying the man's somber call for repentance, citing the Day of the Lord that was now upon us. Such forecasts had always made me nervous. It seemed the magic thing my faith was supposed to do for me had not yet occurred. I was too sick now to nurse my apprehensions, though, and mostly I just wished for the babies to come, for my body to be returned to me, for Saturday night to be over and done with.

Joe's eyes kept steady on the screen, and sometimes I heard him whispering to the Georgia preacher, "You better check your bible, my friend." The Reverend Joe found much to despise in the preacher's messages, yet he didn't stop watching. He said the invention of the television had been prophesied about in the book of Revelations and that there was nothing to stop Christ's coming now. He said God's hand guided the onward march of technology. "They already have color television in the works," he told me. His eyes were trimmed in red and his face was gray-pale. I asked him what kind of sleep he'd gotten lately, imagining him slipping away from our bed in the middle of the night, me sleeping on, not knowing. But he impatiently waved my concerns away, predicting that by the decade's end, there would be a television set in every American household. "This," he waved his hand towards the television, "is the next prophet."

I shampooed the rug in the living room, separating the carpet fibers with a metal comb. The windows were washed with vinegar and water, the kitchen floor with ammonia. Laney brought up test biscuits each day at noon except Friday when she finally admitted she was tired out from her cooking and thought she'd just rest up on her sofa downstairs. I brought her a glass of iced tea and sat with her for a while, listening to her breathing ease off in sleep.

"I want to go home," I said to Joe when I returned to our apartment.

"I'll not abandon my calling, Marianne," he said, and I could tell the thought of my leaving on my own had not occurred to him. I wondered what kind of casserole Dottie Bligh might bring him if I left. I pictured her standing in the doorway of our apartment with a pan of chicken and dumplings, still warm. There would be a string of church ladies stopping by for weeks, apple pies and biscuits, homemade jam.

"I want to go home to have the babies," I said, and he turned once more to me. I thought I had finally reached him, and that now, for a moment, he would understand something of the fear I had been holding.

Joe once said, "I love you, Marianne. I don't know what else to do with you." In those days, he seemed baffled, and in love with that feeling. He thought I was something bigger than I was, and now, he was finding me small yet unmanageable and he didn't know what to do with his disappointment.

It was later that evening, when he came home from yet another elders' meeting and called for me, found me ill in bed and then lay down, the humid warmth of a summer night coming in through the open window. He whispered, "Just don't keep away too long. Don't stay gone. Marianne. Please hear what I'm saying to you."

I made a last quick trip to the market on Saturday morning and spent the day preparing for dinner. I scrubbed potatoes and carrots and toasted bread crumbs for dressing. Paying little heed to the uncomfortable weather, I roasted a turkey and, as the afternoon wore on, the warm smell of a dead bird cooking filled the apartment. I hurried downstairs to check on Laney, still tired out, and scrounged around her china cabinet for serving pieces. Later, I dressed. All that was left to do then was to carve the turkey and set the biscuits out. I'd also made a Jell-O salad and, besides the boiled potatoes and carrot-and-raisin salad, I'd heated a can of Laney's green beans, found in the back of her pantry among a row of various canned goods, the tops dusty.

The Reverend Joe had decided we would eat upstairs, the four of us—five, if Laney rallied—cramped around our own tiny dinette, though Laney had offered her larger, more elegant dining table downstairs. He seemed better now, calmer. "You're better now," I said and he looked at me, surprised. "I didn't know," he said, smiling, "that I was in need of improvement." Soon, it was time for the Blighs to arrive.

"I've just been *dreaming* about this evening," Dottie said, stepping into the house. "We don't see each other nearly enough." She kissed me, leaving sticky lipstick smudges on my cheek. The men slipped by us, into the living room. "My dear, you're beautiful," Dottie said.

I smiled, reaching to clasp her outstretched hands. For this evening, I had chosen to dress my part, digging up a delicate pink maternity dress with an enormous bow across the top of my belly. The dress was a bit snug, and too warm, but one of the church ladies had given it to me, a hand-me-down, and though it was a bit precious for my taste, I could think of no better occasion.

"It *is* a fine evening, isn't it?" Dottie bounced a little in her pumps, following me into the living room. "Perhaps later we could take our coffee outside." She turned to me. "You have lawn chairs? Oh, you simply must. Martin and I set our chairs out most evenings, just to watch the darkness. Star-gazing is what you would call it if we were a few years younger." She laughed to herself. "What's it, Martin? Was it the hardware store in Watson where we picked those up?" Martin grunted and shrugged and Dottie waved the thought away. "No matter." She looked down at her hands and I knew she was searching for a drink. I rose to fetch iced teas.

"There's this preacher with a television show out of Atlanta," Joe was telling Martin when I returned, Dottie perched next to him like a show bird. Martin fiddled with a set of ceramic cats on the coffee table. He set them down, facing outward, and hooked his fingers together, gazing up at Joe dully.

"Broadcasts daily. A few minutes of devotions, but mostly, there's the teaching. And a lady who plays the piano, another who sings. He closes everyday with her singing *What a Friend We Have in Jesus.*" Joe leans in, earnest. "He's half wrong, everything he says. The world is hungry to be fed and he's up there, telling of the law." He took a sip of his tea. "Nothing of true salvation. Not a word that might bring the average man a taste of pure peace."

"I've seen the fellow," Dottie butted in. "I get such a charge out of watching those shows. I said, Martin, what we need to do is get that preacher a television set. Him and his wife, with those babies coming soon. I still marvel at the thought. *Twins.*"

"That preacher's out of Atlanta." Joe tapped the coffee table with his fingertips.

"They have the educational shows," Dottie cooed. "Music is good for children. As edifying as moral instruction."

"God almighty broadcasting across the country," Joe declared.

Martin sat by, adjusting the strap on his watch and staring at the television screen. He said, "I can't see how it will happen, Joe. Everything you're saying about the Lost coming to Christ by the television set. The world at its end." He shook his head.

"Logical conclusion," Joe said. "Just look about you, it's happening."

"I *adore* Lucille Ball," Dottie was saying, releasing Joe's sleeve. "You can't help but love her."

"That's what it is," Martin said. He set his glass down and turned to my husband, hunkering down for serious talk. "You're talking about some crazy new world order, Joe. You're dreaming, boy. I hate to say it." Martin looked at Joe. I think these were the most words the man had ever spoken in my presence. I tried to catch Joe's eye but he wouldn't glance my way. "You keep talking like this and you'll be replaced. The elders have talked it over. I hate to say such things, but it's coming. You and your lovely wife," he glanced at me, "and those babies." His fish-eyes settled on my enormous pink middle. "I hate to say it," he said again.

"Should all the world be converted," my husband declared.

"Joe," I started, rising.

"Just think of your family," Martin said.

I excused myself to the kitchen and there I stirred the green beans, then sat down at the dinette to rest a moment. I tried to picture Joe on the television screen, preaching to the world. My feet hurt, my back hurt, a long dull pain that pulled at my lower back. My toes were swollen inside my pink shoes, my ankles puffing out over the tops. The Reverend Joe on the television, grappling about salvation. I would bring Laney home with me; there was no other way. I dreamed of it, of the porch swing and the brilliant cool blue of a mountain autumn day, the mountains before me sprinkled with a million dots of color, of gold and purple and red. I pictured myself there, Laney and my mother, my sisters, beside me. My huge belly was gone and the babies were secure there, tended to by my own mother.

After a few moments, Dottie appeared. "I bought the television set," she confessed, picking up a spatula by the sink and staring at it like she didn't know what it was. "Martin didn't even know I had done it until the bill came. By then, it was too late. There was nothing he could do."

I nodded. "You're in love with the Reverend Joe."

She balked. "Oh, no, Marianne. No."

"You are," I said, "and it's okay."

Dottie tried to protest, but I looked square at her and she quieted. I was thinking of the golden boy lost in the lake years ago. I wondered what would have become of me if he'd come out of the water, if I'd lost my shyness and ventured a few words. If we'd grown to love each other and marry, if I had kept my love for Joe as thin as sunshine coming through the window.

Later, we went out to take our coffee on the lawn. We had no chairs, but we stood out there, gazing upward, at the stars. I clasped my hands over my belly and studied my husband's face, tilted toward the heavens. We stood beneath the black sky, me feeling the vastness of space, Joe watching the television rays beaming across, unseen.

# The Neighbors

Russell Cartwright celebrated the first summer storm of his retirement by stepping onto the beach to breathe in the electric thrill of hot clashing cold. The air was singed, the water a willing party—a surge of charged matter shot through Russell's body. Earlier that day, his neighbor George Parting had unexpectedly come into a large sum of money. George and his wife read the number on the check over and over again, trying to believe this had happened to them.

Russell's lightning strike occurred on a span of beach close to the A&P he had owned until just a few days earlier, and the store was only a couple of blocks away from his house, given to him and Lenni years ago as a wedding present from her parents. When he smelled the approaching storm through the screened window, he gave little thought to stepping outside, walking across the lawn, bordered with Lenni's hydrangeas and dahlias, and down the two blocks that separated their home from the Atlantic. He lay on the sand, in submission to the great rain that soaked him immediately, not like a rain at all but instead like a spilled ocean. He watched the lightning thread down the dark sky, followed by the angry snarl of thunder. When it struck him, the electricity followed charged water particles webbed upon the sand, seeping up through his shirt, and caused his hair to instantly turn white. Muscle spasms and confusion set in, along with partial amnesia; Russell lay in the hospital bed the next day and tried to keep a thought in his head. Mainly, he wondered who was this woman who leaned over him holding a plastic cup of water to his lips. She smelled like a coin, warm and moist in the palm of his hand, but he couldn't trust his senses since the water tasted like copper.

He closed his eyes and waited for a kiss because he thought a kiss was possible. This woman clutching a water cup in her hand might stoop over and drop a kiss onto his lips and then his plan was to hold her there with his good arm, but she didn't. What she did was set the cup on a table and look doubtfully down at him. She spoke and Russell listened closely but he couldn't determine what the words were and for a moment, he thought he was trying the wrong language.

He was discharged from the hospital two days later. Lenni took him home and set him in front of the television. She switched it to a tennis match and said, "There." If he needed anything he should let her know, she told him. Then, she sat down to flip through a magazine at the kitchen table, sipping hot coffee and trying to get her mind on what tasks most needed her attention. Lenni didn't know what to make of her husband's accident and was more annoyed than distraught. She picked up the phone to call their daughter, who lived in Pennsylvania with her children and her husband, but then thought she should wait. Michelle was a working mother, so it was unlikely she would be home before six. Besides, there were other things to do; the house needed cleaning. Lenni had thought of filling the legs of an old pair of pantyhose with rice and then shoving them into the cracks around the sofa to anchor the new green slipcover in place. She'd mail-ordered it to spruce up the place, along with crisp white lampshades and cranberry-colored placemats for the table. Though she admired the look of the lampshades and the placemats, she was disappointed with the slipcover—it puckered and pleated and dragged to the carpet. She turned her coffee cup in her hands and thought of other ways to fix it.

Next door, the Partings stood in their similarly old house, filled with brown furniture and oatmeal-colored walls. Lydia and George were older than the Cartwrights; in fact, they were older than most of the people they knew. While Lydia enjoyed the look of nice furniture in magazines, and though she still dreamt of a velvet sofa she had seen in a shop window years ago, she and George valued thrift. She would never spend good money on anything as frivolous as a slipcover or buy a new thing until the old thing was completely worn bare and unserviceable.

The two sat on their still serviceable couch and looked at the cashier's check, counting and recounting the number of digits before the decimal. There were six, beginning with a nine—nearly a million dollars. George and Lydia had never seen money like that and the whole business made them nervous. His anxiety had begun with the phone call from the attorney, which scared George a little, knowing how everyone was out to sue everyone else these days. The attorney's explanation of George's cousin's will lessened George's concerns, though he would still say that whatever the business, lawyers made him nervous. Then there was the drive to the attorney's office in Savannah that morning. Lydia hated to be on the interstate, repeating the exit number to herself and noting where the rest stops were, where they might stop for coffee. Now the check was in their possession and they both half-wished they hadn't bothered with the trip.

"Well," George said, "I suppose it should go in the bank."

They discussed further what to do with the money. Their grandchildren were grown, really too old to be spoiled with money, and their children were successful in terms of wealth—one was a stockbroker and the other was married to an orthodontist.

"There's the church," Lydia said.

"And the babies," George added, meaning their five great-grandchildren, with two more on the way. "We could save it," he considered. It was what they had always done with money.

Lydia fingered the doily she'd finished crocheting earlier in the day. She smoothed it across her lap and watched her husband light a cigar. The check lay on the coffee table. She wondered if she should give up crocheting. It was a complicated pattern, almost too much for her eyes, and now that it was done, she couldn't think of anything else to make. George thought about how he would explain the large amount to the teller. He knew it would look suspicious. It didn't occur to him that other people often deposited huge amounts of money, that professionalism prevented the teller from saying anything even if she did think it suspect. What was an old man like him doing with so much money? Sudden money seemed fit only for a younger man. Yet George's fingers couldn't stop touching the check; he couldn't help himself from looking at the number once and again, seeing his name there. They spent the rest of the afternoon that way, thinking of different things, and, after a while, they went out for a hotdog, Lydia pausing by the door to strap on her good walking sandals.

It was nearly seven o'clock when Lenni helped Russell with a bowl of soup and a dessert of strawberry Jell-O. He ate sloppily and watched Lenni so closely she became nervous and dropped the spoon. "Oh, look what's happened," she said. She didn't often wonder what Russell was thinking, but she wondered now, and not knowing unsettled her. She placed him again in the den and returned to the kitchen, opened the refrigerator, and, depressed by leftover meatloaf, she decided to go out. For a moment, she wondered if it was okay to leave Russell on his own, but then, glancing back at him, completely still in the easy-chair, his face utterly blank, she decided it would have to be all right. She wouldn't stay away long.

At the hotdog stand—a place too common for the tourists to

bother with—she ordered a cheeseburger and sat down at one of the outdoor plastic tables with her dinner. She didn't notice her neighbors approach until Lydia touched her shoulder and said her name. Lenni smiled at them, wiping her chin with her napkin. Lydia was such a quiet, bland-faced woman that Lenni never quite knew what to say to her. George, standing back a few paces with a tray littered with empty french-fry cartons and ketchup-smeared wax paper, asked how she was. Why, she was just fine, she answered. Eating by herself? Yes, well. How's Russell? The Partings had heard about his accident.

"Russell's fine," she answered. Lenni found his strike slightly embarrassing and had dreaded the inevitable questions from neighbors and friends, the other year-round residents of the island who had been shopping at Russell's A&P for thirty years or more. She was beginning to think she shouldn't tell her daughter about it at all, or at least not until she and her family visited at Thanksgiving. Lenni couldn't think how she would explain what had happened. What was Russell doing out there, on the beach, during a storm anyway?

"He's home, watching sports," Lenni continued, smiling.

"Ah, good fellow," George said, bouncing the tray a little as if he meant to make it nod.

But Lydia wanted to know the particulars of Russell's injuries. The article in the newspaper had been brief, only saying that Russell Cartwright, resident of Jekyll Island, had been struck by lightning and, after a two-day stay at the hospital, was now recuperating at home.

"Is he badly hurt?" she asked.

"Oh, no," Lenni answered. "He's just a little disoriented, a little weak. Really, he's doing just fine. Soon, he'll be as good as new." She paused to take a sip of her drink. Lydia watched her, expecting more, and Lenni struggled to think of something else to say. She thought of how she had left Russell, vacant-eyed, caught in a strange fog. It was frightening to see her husband that way, and also somewhat annoying—why had Russell done such a thing, anyway? And now, she was the one who would be called upon to explain it. In a way, his accident opened up their marriage to the world, exposing the flaws, the distances between them.

"He's thought about traveling some, you know," she finally said, setting her Styrofoam cup down. Lenni had always dreamed her husband would surprise her with a trip to somewhere spectacular. "He wants to do some sightseeing."

Lydia nodded, smiling, though she wondered at this. Russell Cartwright was not the sort of person to enjoy travel. He was a quiet man who spent much of his time on the side porch with a newspaper and a cup of coffee. He didn't talk so much as he nodded. *Hello* was a nod. *Have a good day*, another nod. *I see you're watering your wife's impatiens again*, sigh, then nod. Lydia had long been curious about their marriage—Russell so quiet and unaffected, Lenni so showy, so many flowers.

"Yes, that's right," Lenni continued. "He's even spoken of going overseas; can you believe that?" Years ago, she had seen an advertisement in a magazine: *Travel historic Europe in luxury!*

Lydia thought of Russell standing behind the cash register at the A&P, watching the surveillance mirrors with one eye as he rung up the groceries, his hair combed flat against his forehead. He hardly seemed like a man who would care to dine in a Parisian café.

"He wants something of a second honeymoon," Lenni said. "Imagine, after forty-three years!" She sighed. It was a bitter thought. Besides their honeymoon to Niagara Falls, she and Russell had done little traveling. His legs cramped in long car rides and he thought traveling by air was too expensive and too public.

"He's retired now," she went on. "He sold the store." Of course, the Partings knew this, and Lenni knew they did, but she was preoccupied, thinking of a trip. Lenni had always hoped to travel. She wanted to take in the *Arc de Triomphe* in Paris, to float along the back canals of Venice, to stroll the cobbled streets of London.

"Of course," Lenni said. "We'll wait to go on the trip. We'll have to wait until he's stronger."

Lydia watched Lenni finger the straw in her drink. She seemed to not know what to do with her hands, touching her drink, her hair, the wrapping on her cheeseburger. Twisting a napkin in her hands, she fashioned it into a cord and twined it around her finger.

"That accident changed everything about him," she said, uncoiling the napkin and dropping it onto her tray. She looked past George and Lydia, into the yellow sky.

"Changed him?" Lydia asked. "Changed everything?"

"I mean us," Lenni answered. "It changed us."

Lydia waited a moment for Lenni to explain, but she only shook her head, shrugging, and dropped her hands into her lap. "I don't know what I'm saying," she said. "I'm tired. I've hardly slept."

"Of course," Lydia said. "You must be exhausted."

No one knew what else to say. George was stiff from holding the tray and Lydia's legs were bad to start throbbing if she stood for too long. Both wanted to return home. They planned to walk slowly and listen to the familiar sounds of the surf, rather like a type of quiet. They wanted to sit on the edge of the beach and let the sun drop behind them—they wanted to think about the stillness of their lives and to remember things. To be outside of their house, away from the check, yet thinking about the money. Each secretly thought of things to buy—each was afraid to tell the other. Lydia suspected Lenni, who sat staring off at the ocean drive rooftops, pinking up in the setting sun, was not telling them everything there was to tell, that there was more to Russell's condition than she was letting on. She thought he must be badly hurt, and she couldn't help but wonder how well Lenni was caring for him. But she knew Lenni would say no more, so she nudged George, telling Lenni they needed to get going, and they left her there, the wind from the ocean pulling at her hair.

Soon after the Partings disappeared down the pathway to the beach, Lenni threw her food away and left, stopping at the A&P

on her way home. The new owners seemed happy to see her. They asked about Russell's recovery.

"He's regaining his strength," she said, echoing what she had told the Partings. "He's going to be just fine."

Harry, the thirtyish stock boy who had a talent for arranging the produce in attractive displays, was anxious for her to assess what he had done with the avocados. Poor Harry, she thought as she moved to the door, slipping a small hypnotism how-to book, from the rack of mini-horoscopes and crosswords, into her pocket. A plan was working itself out in her mind. A plan so strange, so unlikely, Lenni did not think of it directly; she instead concentrated on Harry. He was still used to pleasing Russell—avocados were high-priced produce. As the door closed behind her, she set off for home, touching the book in her jeans' pocket. It was the first item she'd stolen since the store changed hands and she was surprised at herself.

While Lenni was gone, Russell hadn't moved from his spot in front of the TV, partly because his left leg was weak and felt prickly and warm, as though it was asleep, on the verge of restoring sensation, and partly because it never occurred to him to change his location. He was lost in a series of wakeful dreams, unable to fully distinguish between the real and the imagined. Each thought felt solid and true. Between glimpses of the feeding troughs and chicken wire he recalled from when he was a boy, growing up on a turkey farm, he saw the lightning that changed him. He remembered a time when he was very young. He had been lost walking home from town and happened upon a small clapboard house, on the edge of it all. He knocked on the door and a woman answered. She was smaller and plainer and poorer than Russell's mother, and her children were different children, not he and his sisters. It was a strange experience for young Russell, like déjà vu or stepping into another person's life, and for a time, he thought of brothers and sisters who didn't exist. He believed the tiny house was magic, that if he went back out onto the long, empty dirt road, he'd find nothing but a few live oaks at the end, Spanish moss held in their boughs like drooping hair.

In his dreams, he caught several flashes of Lenni, younger and thicker, but did not connect them to each other or to the skeletal-thin woman who came home at last and took the empty soda can from his hand, turned off the television. He knew this was the woman he loved, a knowledge all the more urgent for everything he couldn't remember. He didn't know her name, but as she leaned over him and guided him out of the chair and down the hallway to their bedroom, he looked at her and wanted to touch her face. Instead, he lay in the dark next to her and listened to her breathe, and began to remember that one thing—the steady in and out of her breathing as she slept.

The Partings were silent as they sat side by side in the sand, the beach growing darker, the waves crawling up the sand, drawing nearer, and they continued to sit, both waiting for the other to say it was time to leave. Lydia had always held a gentle love for her husband, but now, as they were suddenly old, suddenly wealthy, she wanted some time for herself. This is my chance, she thought, to remember what I will. She and George finally returned to their home that evening, after walking in the dark with only the moon's light and that of the hotels across the way. She closed her eyes in bed and wondered if she might become a widow, how that would be. She heard George let out his tiny groans in sleep, as if there was something painful about drifting off, and she imagined he was another man. There had been one. He was three years younger than Lydia. In her mind, he was still very young, had not changed, never would. He wore spicy, lightly woodsy cologne, unlike the other boys, and his cheek was always fresh-shaven, as if to indicate some sort of gentleness he was choosing over stronger, more mannish tendencies. He once borrowed his brother's Studebaker and parked it in the middle of an empty field that was resting between cotton and tobacco. He had wanted to make love to her there, in the back seat, but Lydia refused. Now, she thought she should have complied. It wouldn't be as simple as a different man lying next to her now. There would have been different children, a different house. She could be lying in any bed, next to another ocean, or anywhere in between.

She rose early in the morning, leaving George asleep in bed, and went to the kitchen to make scrambled eggs and strong coffee. Leaving both on the stove for George's breakfast, she went out onto the beach by herself. She half-expected to see the young man from long ago.

When she returned home, she looked at the small boxwood bushes on either side of her front door, and she didn't want to go inside. Instead, she turned and walked next door to the Cartwrights'. She remembered how Lenni had fidgeted the night before and had spoken of a trip, how she had looked far off and murmured something about great changes, and Lydia worried about Russell's well-being. Lenni had said he was recovering nicely, but Lydia could not convince herself this was true. She was sure something was not quite right.

She thought of peering through a window. She hesitated—she didn't know what was the matter with her. Never before had she been a busybody and yet here she was. She still thought of the young man from her youth, and somehow, he was the reason she stepped carefully around Lenni's freshly planted zinnias, making her way to the west window at the back of the house where she looked through the slats of mini-blinds, and saw Russell in bed, alone. He was naked, lying on his side, his back turned to her. She caught her breath at the sight of his hair, as white as the starched pillowcase beneath it, and she stepped back a half step, yet didn't leave. Lydia thought, I shouldn't be seeing this. But she stayed a moment longer, then another moment, and didn't leave until he turned to the window, opened his eyes, and smiled.

Russell didn't recognize the woman, but he wasn't alarmed by her presence. He was still caught in snippets of dreams and illusions, memories and fantasies. Lydia's face behind the mini-blinds became a swirling image, floating through his conscious, his subconscious, him lying there, hoping Lenni would come to him.

But Lenni was in the kitchen, sipping coffee and reading. *Hypnotic suggestion must take place in an atmosphere of care and trust. Dim the lights, speak softly, and ask your patient to focus on a spot on the wall or on a photograph. Explain to him that he will enter a state of acute relaxation.*

She read the tiny book over two cups of coffee, and when she was done, she smoothed its cover and slipped it under the silverware caddy in the drawer. Lenni could not stop thinking about what she had said to her neighbors the night before about taking a trip to Europe. She remembered Lydia's reaction to the idea, how she had questioned her, how she had watched her so carefully. Lenni knew she didn't believe her.

She had found the tour group's advertisement in the back of a women's magazine she dawdled over while waiting for Michelle, only a little girl then, to awaken from her nap. There, squeezed between advertisements for beauty creams and nursing bras, was the enticing offer: *Travel historic Europe in luxury!* Lenni wrote to the address listed and requested a brochure. When it arrived, she pored over the glossy photos of the old continent's shining accomplishments: Big Ben and the Eiffel Tower, the Roman Coliseum and the Sistine Chapel. *Travel historic Europe in luxury!* She left the brochure out on the dresser for Russell to notice, but weeks went by without a word. When she asked him about it, he waved her off, saying it wasn't practical. Where was her head?

She spent years planting dahlia bulbs and dreaming of that trip. When Russell was away at the store, often for more than twelve hours in a day, and all the years that Michelle was growing up, and after she left, Lenni planted zinnias and verbenas and impatiens. The more Russell was gone, the more he dismissed her, coming home silently from work, slipping out again early in the morning; the more he sat on the side porch and watched the traffic go by, closed off from her, the more she planted. The flowers filled the yard and grew in the empty spaces of their marriage. She had only mentioned the trip once since Russell announced his retirement. He turned slowly to look at her, saying, *What, now? Are you saying you want to go on a trip* now?

Her hands trembled as she took the phone book from its drawer and opened it, neatly creasing the cover back. She hadn't answered him, had only slipped away, embarrassed by his response. But now, as she flipped through the pages, looking for the airlines listings, she thought of what she should have said: *I want this trip, Russell, and you should want to take me.*

Lenni found the listing and made the call, requesting two seats on a flight to Paris, to depart from Atlanta on Friday afternoon. That was four days from today. She stood looking out the kitchen window, the phone still in her hand. The morning was growing hot and her daylilies by the mailbox shimmered in the heat. Above them lay the sky that always looked sea-washed to her, as if the ocean flooded the heavens every night while she slept. She had grown up in this very house, but it had grown smaller in the years since she was a baby. She had stood on the edge of the Atlantic too many times, looking across and wondering what was on the other side. Europe, her father had said, disgustedly—he had spent three years fighting there. But Russell had never been and there was no reason for him to despise it, no reason to shrug off her requests for so long.

Lenni wiped the counter and thought, this will be easy. She made another call, explaining to the landscapers the changes she wanted made to the lawn, and stepped into her shoes, preparing to go out and pick up a cantaloupe for a soup she wanted to make. She already knew she'd steal something, and it relaxed her to think about what it might be. A travel-size can of shaving cream, maybe. Perhaps a pouch of chewing tobacco. With the hypnotism book, she'd broken her rule about never stealing anything she would actually use, and she was anxious to set herself right. In the past, she had lifted, among other things, a collection of Elvis Presley key chains and a half dozen seashell bracelets, the kind the tourists bought.

    Russell heard Lenni calling to him, and though he didn't understand most of her words, he knew what the sound of the front door closing meant—she was gone. He tried to say her name, but he couldn't. He was growing stronger in some areas: he was able to walk and now had control over his arms, though his left forearm still had a buzzing sensation when he stood near the refrigerator or the stove or the radio. His short-term memory was more acute, though things from the past were still disconnected from each other. He remained unable to talk. He lay still for a while, but then rose, wandered into the kitchen, and bit into an apple, standing as he ate.

He and Lenni left Friday morning. While they were gone, Lydia and George sat on their side porch and watched in amazement as the landscapers tore the Cartwrights' yard apart. They brought a backhoe, with steel tracks, George pointed out to Lydia. He was taken with the machinery, warning Lydia that if the operator made the smallest error, coming too close, they might loosen the foundation of the house, or tear out the ornamental cherry tree— George knew Lenni Cartwright would be up in arms over that.

    Lydia nodded. "Yes," she said. "Lenni would never let them get away with that."

    The concrete walkway connecting the driveway to the front door was pulled from the ground and its great chunks were hauled away in the back of the pick-up. Then, the steel poles that used to hold up Lenni's mother's grapevine were extracted, complete with their concrete foundations. The entire lawn, flowers and grass and all, was torn up and the earth below tilled. Even the cherry tree was uprooted. George wouldn't let that happen without flagging down the head landscaper and asking, "Are you sure, now? That's a terrible expensive tree." George waved his arms through the air. "Pretty, too," Lydia said, agreeing with her husband, a bit nervous to be on Russell's lawn, thinking of what she'd seen. She wondered if Russell had told Lenni about the incident, if he had been able to. She had never seen a man so lost.

The landscapers adjusted their ball caps and nodded at the Partings, assuring them they were following Mrs. Cartwright's express directions. George argued for a moment, then retreated, telling Lydia what a shame it was. He told her it was awful to waste that kind of money and Lydia looked at him—it was the first thing he had said about money since the day they had gone to Macon to accept the check. George had taken it to the bank and nothing more was said. Now, the uprooting of the cherry tree bothered him so much, he went inside and filled a glass with rum and water. He drank it down, then set the glass on the counter and brought his thick fingers to his lips.

"We've grown old," he said.

"Yes."

"Hardly seems worth it."

Not sure of what he meant, she took several long seconds to respond and when she did, he had already poured himself another drink.

"It's a beautiful tree," she said.

He looked back at her and Lydia could see herself reflected in him. He was disappointed and it was the exact mirror of her own feelings, duplicated perfectly and perfectly backwards. Our pain is in simple symmetry, she thought.

The spending began that night. Lydia rose sometime past midnight to find George sitting in the living room in his underwear. He had the phone cradled to his ear, the television turned onto the Home Shopping Network. He ordered a set of sixty-four hunting knives. "Well, okay. That's just fine," she said. The next day she took a bus to Macon and bought a twelve-place setting of new china at Dillard's. Afterwards, she sat down at a gourmet coffee shop and sipped a three-dollar cup of cappuccino. George bought new golf clubs. Lydia bought a Mercedes.

There was a discussion over the car. George said, "Well, Lydia, what do you mean, buying a new car?" She said, "I mean to drive it, George." He was red-faced and sweating; Lydia had to turn away. "You'll return the car," he said, but she didn't. She thought of the Studebaker from long ago and the money that had come and allowed her to purchase this pale-blue machine with white leather on the inside and such power under her foot. She drove it three blocks to the public access beach and parked it carefully between the painted lines. Walking onto the beach, she thought about how late she was. She noticed nobody was looking at her, not even glancing her way, and she thought, maybe I don't exist anymore. Looking down at her wrinkled hands, she told herself she should be wiser than this. She thought of Lenni and Russell in Europe and wondered if Lenni had walked into the bedroom after Lydia left and slipped out of her clothing, leaving it all in a careless pile on the floor. If she had crawled into bed beside her husband and pressed her bare body against his. She and George had once lain together like that, many early mornings when the children were little, and whispered together how they would like to stay that way for the morning, for the entire day. They had been so happy, those mornings. But that was long ago and there was no use remembering such things now. George had said it himself—they were old. She looked at the ocean, the foam on the waves like crinkled white tulle and she put her fingers to her hair, cut short and permed, but she tried to think of it long and floating around her face like seaweed. She *had* been young.

George bought new fishing poles. Lydia drove the Mercedes to Savannah and shopped the boutique shops downtown, hoping to find the velvet couch she had seen in a shop window so many years ago. She spent the day there, wandering in and out of shops, and didn't come home until past dark. When she returned, George was sitting in the living room with no lights on, bewildered and a little fearful of Lydia's behavior. It was unlike her to spend the day in Savannah by herself, to come home so late. He said he didn't know what she might do next.

At the Cartwrights' house, the landscapers were almost finished planting the new grass. There was not a flower remaining in their yard. George stood on the porch, watching the landscaper seed the lawn, and wondered at his wife, away again, still looking for a velvet sofa. She had been searching for a week now, and George didn't understand what the problem was. Surely there was nice furniture to be found someplace in Georgia. Lydia said no. Not like what she wanted. The lawn next door was nothing but mud. There were two people working, one pushing the seed spreader and the other laying out the straw. Though all the damage had already been done, George felt compelled to cross the lawn, careful to avoid the newly seeded spots, and ask the chief landscaper one more time, "Does Russell know about all this?"

Across the sea, Russell was slowly coming to his own mind as Lenni took him from the Eiffel Tower to the Louvre, that was Paris, and then, they rented a car and drove through the yellow and green French countryside until they were in England where there were sheep and hills and Stonehenge, more hills, then finally the sea, set on rocks instead of sand like at home. In the hotels at night, Lenni tried out the magic of hypnotic suggestion, attempting to convert his consciousness to a pleasant floating, but he resisted. He spoke his first word, "Lenni," and then, "please." She turned away, planning the next day's itinerary. They would tour the Nordic countries in a week, from Denmark to Finland, then take a train to St. Petersburg.

Lenni wanted Russell to believe that their forty-three years had been happy ones. She thought losing your memory could be the greatest gift. Lenni wished it for herself, but if she could at least change Russell's memories, then her own would be changed. She took him to Russia, and it was in Peterhoff, near the tiers of cascading fountains, that he held her wrist and whispered, "I love you."

Russell had been trying to smell her hair, had been angling to lie close to her at night, and when the words bubbled up, he tried them right away. He said them again and again, following her down the stone path, over the miniature steel bridges, around the pared trees, behind the bushes where he grabbed her, both of his arms strong again. "I love you, I love you." Finally, he kissed her and Lenni cried. She had never known how sad it would make her, all these years gone by.

They stayed in their hotel room in Saint Petersburg for three days as Russell's language returned, chunks of words at a time, all of it coming back, as if it was an ice storm melting, breaking away in pieces, turning to water and pouring out. Lenni called their daughter and explained to her about the accident. She promised everything was fine, that she would call her again when they returned home. "I just thought you would want to know," she said.

She put the phone down and turned to Russell who was watching American movies dubbed over in Russian on the television, and she said, "Tell me what you remember." He told her of the time when he was very young and became lost, following a dirt road. He explained how he had come to the small white house with the mother and the children and how she had given him bits of canned sausage and beets at their table. After that, he was found, but he knew he could have been born different. "It changes you, you know, to think you could have had a different life."

"Yes," Lenni said, though she didn't. "Go on."

He spoke of the turkey farm, its smell and its filth, of how his father earned his fortune, how he moved away. Russell's mother became ill after a failed pregnancy when he was barely three years old—she'd had to leave Russell with his aunt for a few months while she recovered. "When she returned, I didn't want to go to her," he said. "I suppose I was afraid." These were the stories of his life that Lenni already knew, but she had never heard him speak this way, and it changed him. It changed her to listen. He told her everything he remembered about his life, and the telling reshaped him until he became a tender thing, with thin, frail fingers that seemed more a distinction of youth than of old age. There was a time when Michelle was just a baby and she cried during the night. Russell woke and went to her while Lenni slept on, unaware. He had once fired Joe without telling Lenni, but rehired him the next day. He lay in his bed and dreamt of an old woman coming to peer at him through the window.

"And me? Do you remember me?"

Russell nodded, but said nothing. He began to unbutton her blouse. Lenni remembered what the doctors had said, that the strike had altered the rhythm of his heart and that its new rhythm would continue on, undisturbed, until he died. Inside her husband was a clock, ticking away every minute, on and on. She put her hand on his chest as if to protect the organ inside.

Back in Georgia, Lydia rose late in the morning and went out for a walk. She discarded her thick-soled sandals when she arrived at the beach and rolled up the cuffs of her pants. Walking towards the water, she labored to make her way through the hot sand, past the vacationers, the beach so thick with girls in bikinis, boys in surfer's shorts, past toddlers, diapers sagging with saltwater and sand, young mothers calling after them, smiling.

Close to the water, she lay down, letting the waves come up and over her knees, thinking, this is how the earth disappears into the sea. This is how the ocean comes and claims the land, then the buildings, the people, and finally, the world. She imagined the saltwater taking a piece of her every time it gurgled over her pants, pulling away the sand beneath her ankles. It pulled, this way and that, coming up further this time, at other times, not touching her at all. Closing her eyes to the bright sun, she thought, claim me. She imagined she would fall asleep and the tide would come in and finally, having loosened all the sand around her, it would pull her out to the sea where she would dissolve, floating in the saltwater like amniotic fluid, a soul waiting to be born. She remembered the boy and the Studebaker and she imagined he was out there, on his Studebaker like a ship, ready to rescue her or else to let her be, let her become the sea, as she wanted.

After a while, a tanned young man with muscles in his limbs and a golden-brown beard on his face stopped to nudge her. "Ma'am, are you okay?" But she had fallen asleep. The man tried to shake her awake and a crowd assembled, the bearded man suddenly in charge, telling the others to step back, allow her room, but the tiniest of children slipped through, standing close to her thick white shins, knotted blue veins showing through. Fresh seawater dribbled off their noses and fell on her hands, limp and open. A sudden strong wave came and surged so high, it flooded her, drenching her hair, filling her mouth, but she didn't cough. The bearded man organized the bystanders and she was carefully carried to higher ground—somebody offered his beach towel for her to lie on. Soon, the paramedics arrived in their jeep, beeping their way through the sunbathers, setting to work at once to systemically restart this woman's heart.

George spent the day in Brunswick, looking for a speedboat and all its accessories, surveying the town with a real estate agent—he meant to buy himself some valuable property as an investment, something for his children. When he arrived home and found the house empty, he thought Lydia was getting her hair done, or was out for a walk. He didn't think much of her absence and fell asleep watching the news. He woke late, the house dark except for the television, now playing a sitcom rerun, the canned laughter false and tinny. He knew without looking that he was still alone, that Lydia had not returned. He called the police who informed him his wife had passed on. His first thought was about the newly planted lawn next door. It seemed to be linked to his wife's death, and his second thought was, I'll have to move.

His children came in the morning, but George told them to hold tight; he just needed to pick up a few things. It was the money, he decided. Lydia had worn herself out with the shopping, the searching. The money had made her want things, and the wanting, after so many years of contentment, had been too much at the last. He drove to Brunswick and paid the asking price for a seaside cottage, though he didn't know how he would live there, alone. Thinking of Lydia, he went to look in the shops downtown, spotted a pale blue silk dress in the shop window, and quickly went inside to buy it. He stood watching the sales clerk, a thin man with sharp features, wrap the dress in tissue paper. George paid with cash, counting out the bills one at a time. The clerk smiled. "Must be for a special lady," he said.

He began buying gifts, jewelry for his daughter and his daughter-in-law, for his grandchildren, for the great-grandbabies and the great-grandbabies yet to be born. He bought a shelf of books and a pontoon boat. He made a generous contribution to a church he happened to drive by. At last, the money was spent and George was relieved. He drove home slowly, not happily, but peacefully. It had been a great weight to him and Lydia, having all that money to think about.

Lenni and Russell would not be attending the funeral—they didn't know anything about it, and even if they did, it was unlikely they would have returned. They were wrapped in a tender happiness, traveling by train to Romania, Italy, back to France, then Spain again, Portugal. There they settled for a time and Lenni, pouring Russell a glass of wine in their hotel room, asked him, "Tell me, Russell, why were you out there? In the storm, I mean?" Russell paused for so long, Lenni thought he had forgotten, or maybe he had never known, but finally he answered.

"Watching a storm over the ocean was something I'd never done before. All those years living right there and I'd never seen lightning over the sea." He paused, considering. "As a child," he said, "I saw turkeys. I lived with them, smelled them, watched them, the sound of their warbles the first sound of each day. All the talk was of turkeys. Growing them, slaughtering them, selling them. Living at the beach, it was different." He looked down at his hands, then up again, at Lenni. It almost stopped him, how she tilted her head, how her eyes crinkled a little, how she listened. "There, everything was the ocean, this giant entity, always rising and falling, as big as the world. The storm swelled up that night and I was drawn to it; how could I not be? My God, the way the wind stirred! I wanted to see the lightning split the sky apart, to see it fall into the ocean, to stand back and behold the great powers—storm and sea." Russell stopped, breathing in the salt breeze coming off the beach through the hotel window. "The air smelled like fire," he said, "like melting metal."

Lenni nodded, taking in the words, turning them over in her own mind. She had become greedy that way, snatching the answers he was just beginning to articulate, always wanting more.

"The world turned inside out," she suggested.

"Yes," Russell said, "That's right."

It was September now and the time for them to return home was approaching. Though they had been careful with money, the trip had been expensive and they couldn't afford to stay away much longer. She thought of how the house had changed in their absence, the lawn muddy with new grass, and she wondered how returning would feel.

She said, "I'd like to go for a walk when we get home, before we even bring the bags in. We should go down to the beach, back to our side of the ocean. We should go back there together."

Russell took the glass of wine from her and leaned in to kiss her lips. He tucked a strand of hair behind her ear and lifted her chin with his finger. Drawing her face close to his, he answered.

# *Springtime on Mars* Book Club Discussion Questions

1. Though you shouldn't judge a book by its cover, what were your expectations before reading the book? Did the stories meet these expectations or were you surprised?

2. Susan Woodring plays with family dynamics. What do these different types of families have in common? How are they different?

3. Why do you think "Springtime on Mars" is the book's namesake? Does this story accurately represent the rest of the stories?

4. In "Birds of Illinois," what do the birds symbolize? The meat?

5. Six of the eleven stories are written in the first person. Do you think these stories would be diminished in any way if we didn't have the thoughts of the leading characters?

6. Woodring plays with different fears in "Inertia." What fears are present? Are the characters fearful of different things? Does fear appear in other stories?

7. Compare Jean and Harold's relationship in "Morning Again" to Gladys and Andy's. How would you describe their understanding of their roles in their respective relationships?

8. In "Love Falling," there's a lot of tension in the house. What is the breaking point for Julie? Why does she ultimately decide to leave?

9. Woodring describes the weather with much detail. Why do you think this is, and can you draw any connections between the weather and the temperament of the story?

10. What do you think Woodring is implying in her observations of belief systems: religious, political, and extraterrestrial?

11. Russia makes a frequent appearance in the stories. What do you think it symbolizes?

12. The parent/child relationship is often very strained in the stories. What do you think Woodring is trying show the reader?

13. When Shannon urges Jean to take the triangle IQ test in "Morning Again," she responds, "I've raised three children." What do you think this implies about Jean's values? Shannon's?

14. All of the characters are unique. Is there one in particular you most empathize with? Why or how?

SUSAN YERGLER WOODRING, an award-winning short story writer and novelist, grew up in Greensboro, North Carolina. Upon graduating from Western Carolina University, she spent a year teaching in Vologda, Russia. Susan is a graduate of the Creative Writing MFA program at Queens University in Charlotte. Her short fiction has appeared in a number of literary magazines and anthologies, including *Yemassee, Passages North, turnrow,* and *Surreal South.* In 2006, she won the Elizabeth Simpson Smith Award for Short Fiction and the *Isotope* Editor's Prize. She is the author of one novel, *The Traveling Disease.* Susan currently lives, writes, and home schools her children in western North Carolina.

Cover artist **MENDY MITRANI** is a mixed media artist living in The Woodlands, Texas. Her art has been featured in publications including *Somerset Studios, Somerset Memories, Digital Somerset, Legacy, Scrapbooks Etc., Memory Makers Magazine* and *featured Memory Makers Books, Ivy Cottage, The Leisure Arts Series, and Cantata Books.* She has displayed many art projects at CHA, and The Craft and Hobby Association. She occasionally teaches classes in scrapbooking, collage, and altered art. Mendy lives with her husband, David, two sons, Morry and Max, and Madeline "The Pug." In addition to her work with art, she teaches Kindergarten full time. To find out more about Mendy's art, visit her blog at http://mendytexas.blogspot.com/.

CPSIA information can be obtained at www.ICGtesting.com
Printed in the USA
BVOW041600210613

323981BV00001B/1/P